MW01530719

FRENCH CREEK

Marsha Landreth

AN EVANS NOVEL OF THE WEST

MARSHA LANDRETH

FRENCH CREEK

M. EVANS & COMPANY, INC. NEW YORK

Library of Congress Cataloging-in-Publication Data

Landreth, Marsha
French creek / Marsha Landreth.
p.   cm.—(An Evans novel of the West)
ISBN 0-87131-696-X : $16.95
I. Title   II. Series.
PS3562.A4774F7   1992
813'.54—dc20   92-32277
CIP

Copyright © 1992 by Marsha Landreth

All rights reserved. No part of this book
may be reproduced or transmitted in any form
or by any means without the written
permission of the publisher.

M. Evans and Company, Inc.
216 East 49th Street
New York, New York 10017

Typesetting by AeroType, Inc.

Manufactured in the United States of America

9 8 7 6 5 4 3 2 1

For my grandmother, Nell Benton Bircher, daughter of a homesteader who made the run at the opening of the Cherokee Strip, half-sister to twins Naomi and Ruth who in real life didn't live to see their first birthday. With much love.

Chapter One
Joplin

Joplin leaned against the banister to work an angry kink out of his leg. Seemed that was all he was doing these days. Doc called it R-ride-us, but Joplin knew what it was, all right. Old age, plain and simple. But this was no time to worry over his used-up body. He had something more important to do.

Seeing what had upset Miss Alma was nothing he wanted to do, but there was no one else. Well, the girls said he was the one to do it. Said he had a way with Miss Alma. He liked white folks well enough, but Miss Alma was special. And in all their years together, he'd never before heard Miss Alma cry. Not that she hadn't had plenty of cause. Starting the day that damn yankee Custer killed her brother—one of Mosby's Rangers—up at Front Royal, Virginia, back in 1864.

Like yesterday, Joplin remembered it. The uniformed Confederate, sitting astride his blue roan, asking to speak with her father alone. The Colonel, standing on the vine-shaded veranda as stone-rigid as one of pillars, looked down at the rider. "If you've come to give me word of my son, suh, do so from there. I know you've more pressing matters to attend to."

The Colonel slumped on his hickory cane as he listened. ` The soldier dismounted and, with military deportment, presented Matthew's prized handgun to the Colonel. The Colonel's back was ramrod straight when he reverently took the revolver and thanked the soldier, telling him to take whatever he needed. Then the Colonel walked slowly and proudly into the house. Not one tear escaped his eye.

But it was all show. The Colonel had lost not only his son, but his will to live. Miss Alma took up the reins, seeing to the field slaves in the same efficient manner she cared for the house since the passing of her mama. And Joplin continued to see to the needs of the stabled animals, just as he had for as long as he could remember.

Then, after the war, the Colonel's passing, and the stealing of the plantation for back taxes, Sam took Miss Alma and her three younger sisters in the fancy carriage, leaving him to follow with Mammy in the wagon filled high with trunks. And journeyed all the way to Atlanta where they were taken in by the Colonel's sister.

One by one, Miss Alma married off the girls. By the time little Miss Deedra walked down the aisle, Miss Beatrice had Mammy in her employ, caring for the twin babies, Molly and Cameron.

Her work finished, Miss Alma sold the carriage, outfitted the wagon, and headed West with Sam and himself. Like the fool Joplin knew him to be, Sam believed the tall-talking cavalry recruiter they happened onto in Independence. Sam joined the Tenth and rode off into the sunset to fight wild Indians in Texas. But Joplin was no one's fool, no siree, riding horseback over miles and miles of hot and barren Texas didn't sound as glamourous to him as it did to poor Sam. Besides, he hadn't the heart to leave Miss Alma. She'd lost so much and, even though her pride wouldn't allow her to admit it, Miss Alma needed him.

She needed him mightily. No matter where they went, a thundercloud lingered overhead. When the wagon broke up crossing the North Platte River, Miss Alma—already faced with dwindling supplies—announced her intention of leaving the wagon train and staying in Wyoming Territory. It looked as good as any other place, she said. Joplin knew better, but when Miss Alma's nose climbed high in the air and her back became rigid like the Colonel's, there was no reasoning with her.

The two of them made their way to Cheyenne where Miss Alma found a use for her match-making talents. A certain type of lady needed her organizational skills, but it wasn't exactly akin to marrying off her sisters.

Miss Alma gathered up these ladies and put them under one roof, where their suitors would have to come calling on them. She said it was the only practical thing to do. The women no longer had to work in dirty saloons, traveling from mining camp to mining camp, wondering where their next meal would come from. Miss Alma gave them a home and a family. Even managed to marry off many of them over the years, just as she had her own sisters.

Joplin shook off the past and steeled himself. He limped across the creaky floorboards on unsteady legs and knocked at the door. The sobbing stopped abruptly an eternity of waiting ended with the familiar soft drawl. "Yes?" Miss Alma asked.

Joplin opened the door a crack. She turned her face to the lace-covered window behind the settee. But not before he saw the tear streaks.

"What is it, Joplin? Something wrong?"

He slipped into the room, training his eyes on the hem of her dark blue skirt. "Miss Alma, the girls are—" He left the thought hanging in air.

"The girls are what?" she asked in the same flirtatious yet aloof manner she reserved for her clientele. He didn't like that. It meant she was trying to hide something from him. He was finished pussy-footing around.

"Miss Alma." Joplin took in a deep breath. "What's in

3

the telegram?'' Miss Alma blinked in surprise. And no wonder, his tone was harsher than even he expected. He let it ride, staring right into her eyes with no intention of apologizing.

She looked down at the crumpled paper on the rose-flowered carpet. Struggling to maintain appearances, Miss Alma soared to her considerable height. At about five-foot-seven, she stood eye-to-eye with most men and towered over the rest. Her blond curls were a bit gray these days, but they were still piled high on her head, making her appear even taller.

Miss Alma, pushing her prime, wore only a modest amount of make-up. And even that she didn't need. She was a handsome woman who failed miserably at concealing her full figure beneath the high-necked gray blouse. She placed her hands on a waist only slightly thickened over the years. ''Missy B's twins are coming West for a visit.''

How could that be? As quickly as tired bones allowed, he walked over and scooped up the telegram. He read each word slowly—the only way he knew how—then looked at the address. Mrs. Jonathan Jennings, Rocking J Ranch, French Creek, Wyoming Territory.

Might have known this had something to do with Jennings. They'd been in Cheyenne no more than a couple of years when the giant cattleman walked in. Any blind man could see the sparks fly. The gent's intention of a lovely evening in one of the rooms upstairs slipped suddenly away.

On the night before the smitten rancher from up north headed home, he proposed marriage to Miss Alma. Joplin knew all this because the poor fellow told him later as he drank from the whiskey bottle like a man looking for the bottom. Drinking from the bottle was against house rules, but Joplin let it pass that one time.

Although Miss Alma turned him down, within a year she upped and moved to French Creek with those girls who

4

wanted to go, leaving the establishment to them that stayed. Miss Alma called it branching out. Only good business she said. Joplin knew better.

Jennings called on Miss Alma frequently but discreetly. Each trying to protect the other's reputation. If any of the girls happened to see his comings and goings, they kept silent out of respect for Miss Alma. And Mr. Yates, the postmaster and telegraph operator, and steady client, must have known and kept her secret if Joplin could go by this telegram.

Miss Alma didn't shed one tea as she stood over Jennings' freshly filled grave last month, but she was crying now. A visit from the family. She was going to be found out. Somehow Joplin knew they wouldn't understand at all about Miss Alma. He felt like crying with her. Now that he was recollecting, the last time he saw Missy B's baby twins, one of them was crying.

Chapter Two
Ned

"Buggy comin', Ned." O'Malley, a scrawny red-haired kid, motioned with his chin as he held the calf down.

Foreman Ned Lawson braced his knee behind the calf and thrust the hot iron against its rump until the sweet scent of burning flesh replaced the sizzling of singed hair. He pulled the iron away and looked at the Rocking J brand. Satisfied, he dropped the iron to the dirt. "A buggy, you say?" He looked across the rolling prairie toward the Big Horn Mountains. A buggy headed a ribbon of dust cutting through the valley. A fancy buggy. "Reckon Page is paying his respects?"

O'Malley freed the calf. "He's makin' sure we're not brandin' any of his." Anger gave O'Malley's words a little more Irish than usual. He had been a hand at Page's Circle 8, but was fired for refusing to recut the Rocking J's earmark, a small V, into Circle 8's large U. When the boy—still mostly arms and legs—came to tell Jennings what Page was up to, the old man snatched him right up. Jennings liked a man with staunch principles, and saw promise in the fiery eyes. Ned stared at the buggy. He couldn't imagine why Page would come all the way out to the Rocking J. "It's Page, plain as the nose on my face."

Ned swallowed a grin. Nothing was plain about O'Malley's freckled face, especially his nose. It had peeled like snake skin, and the new skin was already a crisp red. "He knows better. Jennings always bent over backwards to be fair."

" 'Stead of bending over, the old man should've called his bluff. 'Member the Rocking J brand covered poorly with Circle 8 I showed you last fall?"

"A lone calf in a herd of forty thousand isn't worth causing an uproar. The big ranches have to stick together if'n we're to keep barbed wire off the open range."

"And who's going to smooth Page's ruffled feathers now that Jennings's gone?"

It was a good question, one he couldn't answer. "Looks like he's headed toward the chuckwagon." Ned brushed the dust from his chaps and mounted up. He coaxed his blaze-faced sorrel around the calves and their baying mothers and headed toward the chuckwagon.

Melancholy overcame Ned as he rode the greening range. What would happen to all this now that Jennings was gone? He'd roamed over much of the territory, but nothing compared to the beauty along the eastern foothills of the Big Horn Mountains. The basin on the west side was brown and windy, but here in the green valley the mountains acted as a shield against the wind. Where else could a person look for miles in all directions and see so much of Nature's handiwork?

He missed the old man. Jennings was nothing more than a puncher himself, in the beginning. In Texas right after the war, before Abilene and Ellsworth made cattle profitable, while the herds did nothing more than roam and multiply, the visionary Jennings gathered up mavericks at an alarming rate.

He drove his herds first along the Sedalia Trail into Missouri to pick up the Pacific Railroad. Then when the settlers came, he moved West and took the Chisholm Trail to Abilene. When the cattle had to wind their way around the farms, and the Santa Fe Railroad came along, he headed toward Dodge City. After tick fever made the Kansas farmers cranky enough to restrict drives to December through February, Jennings gave up and headed for Wyoming Territory. Not a lick of land could be farmed in Wyoming, or so he thought.

Old Jennings lived long enough to realize some men had been short-changed in the area of common sense. They would scratch any land, even thin prairie dust. Now, all along the eastern foothills of the Big Horns, squatters struggled to eek out a living; each of them wanting a place to call his own where his children could grow like deep-rooted cottonwoods. Maybe he could understand it better if he had a family. But for a man alone there didn't seem much need to have his own land.

Jennings proved that. He built an empire from the sweat of his brow yet his heir, probably a distant relation back in the States, had no desire to even visit the place. A law firm in Kansas City handled all correspondence. To them the cattle represented nothing more than money in the bank.

By time Ned reached the chuckwagon he realized that the buggy wasn't Page's, but rather Miss Alma's. Ned ground-hitched his horse and sauntered over to the used-up cowboy-turned-cook, Shorty, who rubbed his gray whiskers like it helped him think.

"If that don't dadburn beat all," Shorty told Ned, showing a toothless grin. "What's the black-as-a-kettle, wooly-haired bartender from Miss Alma's doin' out here?"

Ned shrugged and pulled up a tender shoot of grass. He drew it through his teeth, tasting the last of the wet spring. He leaned on the wagon's tongue and watched Joplin climb out of the buggy. He couldn't imagine what prompted the old Negro's visit.

Shorty couldn't either. He divided his attention between his frybread and the visitor stumbling up the path. He pinched off pieces and placed them into the greased skillet in record time.

"Mornin', suhs," Joplin said, giving what Ned suspected to be a slight humbling bow. He turned to Ned. "May ayh speak to you, suh?"

Ned led him to a log by the campfire. He moved the cooled coffee over the flame. Ned liked the Negro well enough, liked him better than some of the white folks he knew, but Shorty wasn't the only one itching to know what the man had on his mind. And Ned had a mountain of work to do.

The man didn't seem in any hurry to declare his intentions, but something had to be on his mind. It was a mighty long ride from town for a social call. Ned grabbed two tin cups and waited for the coffee to come to a full boil. When it did, he filled a cup and handed it to the fellow who proved slower than the coffee about coming to the point.

With waning patience, Ned cleared his throat and then sipped his coffee, one eye on the old Jasper. Shorty grumbled his anxiety.

"Mr. Lawson, suh, I've come hyeh to ask yeh help." He wiped rivets of sweat from his broad forehead with the back of his black hand. "Miss Alma don't know I'm hyeh, suh."

"And?"

"Miss Alma got herself in a real fix." Joplin shot the man a quick glance, then looked at the ground. "She has relatives back east she's been corresponding with over the years. Anyhow, she ..." his voice trailed off.

Ned pushed his hat back and leaned in closer to the man. "She what?"

He sighed. "She told 'em...long-time ago, suh, that she was a rancher's wife."

"So?"

"A couple of them are coming hyeh for a visit...coming to the Rocking J, suh."

Ned's coffee sloshed over the sides of his cup as his hand drooped. Alarm must have registered in his eyes from the look mirrored in Joplin's. Didn't take long to realize this had something to do with him. He bobbed his head, listening to Shorty mumble his surprise. "I see. Any way of stopping them?"

The old man's dull black eyes couldn't quite meet Ned's. "They're already on their way, suh."

"What's Miss Alma going...?" Ned noticed Shorty working back closer to the fire for better hearing. "What's this got to do with me?"

"Reckon you could pretend Miss Alma owns the ranch? Let them visit?"

Ned took off his hat and ran nervous fingers through his hair. "Someone's bound to tell 'em about her."

"No one's seen the new owner of Rocking J. Maybe people could be persuaded to think they're them come hyeh to see the spread." Joplin's eyes lit up as he explained how he thought they could pull it off.

Ned scratched his head. "Everyone would recognize Miss Alma, though."

"When they come, suh, we tell 'em that Aunt Missy— Missy, that's what her family always called her—that Aunt Missy had to take a trip down Cheyenne way and that the message didn't come 'til after she left."

"But it's round-up. No one's at the ranch."

Joplin gave a cursory swipe at his dusty shoes, and then meticulously polished them. Stalling for time, Ned suspected. "Maybe I could stay hyeh and care for them, suh."

A fool's errand. "Sorry. Just can't do it. Not my ranch. Can't make that kind of decision for the owners."

Joplin bowed his head, but then looked up hopefully. "Would you walk down to the buggy with me, suh?"

Shorty looked a bit miffed.

Ned nodded. Going to the buggy meant he'd finally be on his way. The campfire snapped and sizzled as Ned threw in his coffee and got up. "Sure thing."

Joplin was silent until far out of Shorty's earshot. "Miss

Alma would skin me alive if she found out I told you this."

"Maybe you shouldn't, then."

"No, I haf'ta."

Ned waited for him to go on. When he didn't, Ned said, "It'll be our secret."

"Jennings was a very...very... good friend of Miss Alma's."

Ned let it sink in. Once it had, the pieces of the jigsaw puzzle fit tightly together and he saw the whole picture. That explained why Jennings'd always slicked up before his weekly trips to town and why he always seemed preoccupied for days after. Not that it was any of his business. "And?"

Joplin shrugged his stooped shoulders. "And back in Cheyenne he'd asked Miss Alma to be his wife. She turned him down because of the girls, but as you see, suh, we moved away from civilization to be near him."

Absorbing all of this took some time. He'd known Jennings almost all his life, since the old man took him in at fourteen. He thought he knew Jennings better than anyone alive, but apparently not. He must have loved her powerfully to ask her to be his bride. And more so not to take another. Ned skirted dangerously close to ignoring his resolve. He kicked a piece of shale through the air as he let the thoughts whirl in his head. What would Jennings do? Whatever she wanted, he reckoned. "All right, they can come."

Suddenly the old black man seemed spry as a rooster. "I'll go tell Miss Alma. You have no idea how happy this will make her. I'll be back here with them in a few days."

"No!" Ned exclaimed, catching the old man's arm. "People here 'bouts know you. Best to keep out of it, so as not to involve Miss Alma...I'll see to them."

Joplin fumbled in his baggy pants and pulled out a crumpled piece of paper and handed it over.

Ned unfolded it. Miss Alma had all but worn out the telegram agonizing over it, he reckoned. "Tell Miss Alma not to fret. If there's trouble, I'll let her know, otherwise tell her to assume everything's smooth as glass." *Most likely smooth as a bull in a glass factory.*

He watched the buggy race away until it was a cloud of dust. With the weight of the world on his shoulders, Ned returned to the cook. He eyed him with uncertainly. He had to squash any notion he might have of blabbing about the strange visit. "Well, Shorty, fine mess we got ourselves in."

Shorty turned back to his chuckbox in disgust. "Reckon I don't know what I've to do with all this here tomfoolery."

Ned picked up the two tin cups and dropped them into the washtub. His lips all but touched the big hunk of yellow wax sticking out of Shorty's good ear as he said, "The way I feature it, somebody's got to take care of these visiting folks. Somebody's got to cook for them. Somebody's got to see to it they don't talk to anybody. Somebody's got to see to it they don't get in any trouble."

Shorty backed away like a man afraid of catching the plague. "You told him they could come?"

Ned nodded.

"And I'm the somebody," his voice cracked, "seeing to it?"

Ned nodded.

"I'd rather be pistol-whipped!"

Ned nodded.

Chapter Three
Cameron

Cameron clawed at his strangling collar as the jerking stagecoach traversed the rain-gutted road. Just out of Cheyenne, and his brown jacket was already covered in trail-dust. He didn't aspire to traveling backwards and he didn't appreciate the way the stubby legs of the fat man butted up against his seat, pinning him to the side. He was taking up all of the bench across from them, that should have been enough for any man, even a fat one. Nor did he relish the way the old man eyed his sister.

"Franklin Page," the fat man said, leaning that much closer as he extended his meaty arm.

"Cameron Stewart, suh," he replied, the sweat of the stranger sliding over his palm. "And this hyeh's my sister, Molly."

"Pleased to make your acquaintance, ma'am." Page tipped his wide-brimmed gray hat greedily.

Molly shifted uncomfortably on the bench in a vain attempt to budge her bustle. "My pleasure, suh."

"Heard tell that the other two passengers were headed up my neck of the woods. You remind me of someone, ma'am, though who, I don't rightly know. You're not a girl a man would see every day."

True, Molly was a beauty, but Cameron didn't appreciate

such talk from a stranger. And knew Molly would be giving him an earful later if he didn't defend her honor. Her disposition wasn't as pretty as her face.

"See here—"

"You all from back east?" Page asked, his beefy fingers reaching for the gold watch inside the vest pocket of his gray three-piece suit.

Cameron had missed his opportunity to tell off the fool. He glanced at Molly. Her face had eased a little hearing her favorite waltz coming from the watch, but her lips pursed as the intruder snapped the lid shut.

"Atlanta," Cameron answered. "Just got of the Union Pacific yesterday, suh." He coughed as he ate dirt. "Didn't realize its luxury then."

Page chuckled. "Still got nearly three hundred miles to go." He winked at Molly. She smiled sweetly, too sweetly. "You stayin' long in French Creek?"

"Thought maybe a month or so." He shot a glance at his sister, she gave no indication of even hearing. But behind her fluid blue eyes, he knew she was stewing.

He would've rather had come alone. She wasn't ruthless enough for the job. But his mother had insisted that his Aunt Missy would be more inclined to give them the needed money if she saw the child who looked so much like her. From the pictures of Aunt Missy as a girl, Cameron would have thought *they* were the twins.

It was a stroke of good luck hearing of Jennings' death just as the rumors started circulating about the crumbling foundation of the shipping business his father started during the embargo years of the war. It had been risky but, while most Southerners were losing everything, he had amassed a fortune. A fortune his mother was swindled out of by the shipping partners after his father's untimely death.

Cameron would stop at nothing to get back what was his, including begging. He hadn't known either his aunt or uncle, but expected it would be easier to get money out of Aunt Missy now that she was a widow. She wouldn't even miss it. Everyone knew how rich cattlemen were.

"Good, be plenty of time to have you to dinner...show you my ranch." Page took off his hat and ran a hand over his glistening bald scalp to collect the sweat, which he wiped on his breeches. "Of course, you cain't see my whole spread or my fifty thousand head of cattle in just one day."

The words were music to Cameron's ears. He looked at the man's chubby fingers. No ring. Perhaps he knew even a better means of getting the money. If Molly were to marry, her husband would be entitled to her shares in the business. A wealthy brother-in-law was much more appealing than a wealthy aunt.

"Surely our visit would be too much of an imposition for Mrs. Page." Cameron watched as the man's eyes strayed Molly's way.

"No worry there, I'm a bachelor man."

Cameron swallowed a lump that rose to his throat. "Molly and I would be delighted to see your estate. Wouldn't we, Molly dear?"

She nodded politely, too politely. But he'd worry about Molly later. "Molly is such a wonderful cook. Perhaps she could fix a picnic basket for our tour." Like a young doe hearing a noise, Molly's head sprang up. She glared at him. They'd always been able to read each other's minds, just about always. But even if she knew he intended to marry her off to this rancher, she wouldn't do anything about it. She knew their situation. Besides looks weren't everything, the man would grow on her.

"Surely the Rocking J has a chicken to spare," Cameron went on. Now it was the rancher's eyes that were fixed on him, but they sparkled. Cameron had used the right approach. Being relatives of another rich rancher was their entree.

"Are you kin to Jennings?"

"He was our uncle," Cameron said with just the right amount of solemnity.

"Your uncle was a very dear friend of mine. I formally extend my condolences."

Cameron smiled his thanks. The trip was working out better than he had hoped.

Chapter Four
Ned

Ned would have felt a sight easier if the main street of French Creek hadn't been so congested. Everyone and his uncle was loitering about. His bad luck that today was the first pleasant one all week.

He left the buckboard in front of Tulley's General Store behind the Circle 8's buckboard so the errand boy could load the supplies. That is, if he ever finished with the Circle 8's order. A drink would hit the spot and he had plenty of time to down a beer at the Egyptian Saloon. Probably two, since the stage wasn't known for it's punctuality, but Ned couldn't afford any slip-ups. So instead of a cold beer to quench his thirst, Ned whistled through a cotton mouth the snappy tune, Sam, the piano player from the Egyptian, was playing loud enough for everyone on the street to hear. He strolled along the boards toward the telegraph office where the stage made it's bimonthly stop.

Uneasiness tore at Ned as he saw one of Page's men slouching against the wall at the telegraph office. Page would hear about the visitors before sundown. He'd probably write to the lawyers in Kansas City and Ned would surely be fired. Ned didn't figure there was anything he could do about it now.

Seeing Ned, he tugged at his hat, showing a shaggy mane

of greasy hair. Ned tipped his hat in return and then leaned against the shady side of the awning post.

"New owner comin', Ned?" he asked after he'd tongued his chew to the other cheek.

Ned gave him a glance, then turned to the commotion in the street. Just a spring wagon. He yanked out his pouch of tobacco and kneaded the slim contents, about enough for one sparse cigarette. If nothing else, his trip to Tulley's was timely. He rolled it. Licking the paper ends only reminded him of his thirst. He struck a match along the awning post, touched the sparkling flame to the tip of his thin cigarette and drew in deeply. "Didn't know you to be the social type, Saint." The no-account was no saint, but talk had it he belonged to a Peter clan. Ned was giving benefit of the doubt believing he had a family anywhere. Most likely he slithered out from under a rock.

"Just know'd how Page feels about the Double D bein' an absentee outfit and all." Saint smiled, showing teeth in need of a good scouring.

Ned couldn't figure why Saint said that, since Page benefitted the most. The Englishman owner of the Double D didn't care a lick about his ranch, besides having a place in the West where he could big-game hunt with all the company he brought every other year or so.

Page got his chance when the Double D foreman started claiming heavy winter losses. Ned thought there might be something to the accusations that the foreman had an after-dark price for cattle, but he suspected a number of the cattle ended up with the Circle 8 brand. Page brought to Duke Darlingsworth's attention the fact that Circle 8 didn't have nearly the winter losses and the next Ned heard, a new foreman was hired under the supervision of the Duke's friend and neighbor, Franklin Page. The Duke was probably sleeping like a baby thinking how his ranch was in such good hands.

Now that old Jennings was gone and the new owners didn't

care a hoot about running the ranch themselves, Ned feared Page would have a pretty free hand in the valley. And seeing Saint here made him mighty curious as to what Page was up to.

"Page got company comin'?" Ned asked, trying to sound disinterested.

"Come to get Page hisself." He spat. The juice splattered against the base of the awning, just missing Ned's freshly greased boots. Ned suspected Saint had missed his mark. "Been down Cheyenne way."

Page was on the stagecoach with his folks! Likely as not, the jig was up before it rightly started. Didn't even have to wait until sundown for Page to hear. But why would Page go away during roundup? Spring roundup for branding calves and fall roundup for beef were the two busiest times of the year, made no sense to be gone then. Had to be pretty important.

"There it comes," Saint said as he spat.

The stagecoach clamored to a halt in front of them, and Ned melted into the wall. He would hunker down and wait to see what was what. Ned's wait was short. The stage barely rolled to a stop before Page sprang out like the knees of an old pair of denims. First old plug Ned knew to prance. Page tugged at the points of his vest as if it could cover the rolls of fat, and then offered a hand to the next descending passenger.

It was a young filly the old plug was trying to impress. Went off and found a non-suspecting bride, did he?

Ned's eyes touched the woman's only a moment before she looked where she was stepping. A tall woman. Ned liked the way she dwarfed Page. Page pulled her in close to make room for the next passenger. The young stranger pomaded his hair, only to push it down with the flat top of his skimpy-brimmed hat.

Ned looked the stranger over as he climbed down. Same

height as the woman, even though his dandy boots had a higher heel. Seemed nervous the way he kept tugging at his cardboard collar. Same blond hair and blue eyes as the woman except his eyes didn't dance. He must have been the bride's brother.

It had been a wasted trip. Relief overwhelmed him. His job was secure. First thing he'd do after telling Miss Alma her kin missed the stage would be to somehow tell her that he couldn't go through with the deception.

Relief vanished as the man ask in a soft drawling voice the location of the Rocking J. And now that he was getting a good look, the woman resembled Miss Alma. Resembled her mightily.

"The Rocking J's just over the hill from my spread." Page still held the young woman's hand as he'd done since helping her out of the stage. The other hand crept possessively around her tiny waist. He helped her up the boardwalk steps and led her to Ned.

Ned stepped toward them trying to keep his wits about him.

"Here he is." Page delivered the woman into his hands. "Now you take care of our Miss Molly, you hear? You see that Miss Molly and Mr. Stewart get over to the Circle 8 as soon as they've settled in."

Ned was totally astonished. A mixed bag of feelings assaulted him. He was happy the cat was still tied in the sack, but the drawstring seemed mighty loose with Page expecting them to visit and all.

"Buckboard's across the street." Ned pointed. "I'll get your gear." He gave Mr. Stewart a nudge. "Rocking J is a far piece up the road. Need to hurry along if'n we're to get back by sundown."

Ned balanced the trunk on one shoulder and carried the carpetbag underarm. Ned bit his tongue to keep from telling this *Mister* Stewart to pitch in. The stranger seemed vexed as he and his sister sat looking around French Creek. Probably wondering how long he had to wait for the hired help to get the baggage on the buckboard.

Ned stumbled as he heard Page tell Saint the hired men were behind him a couple of days. He smelled trouble brewing and hoped it would be directed toward the squatters and not the Rocking J. He tossed the trunk and bag in the back and jumped in lickety-split. It gnawed at him as the easterner waved and called farewells to Page like they were long-lost brothers.

As they passed Miss Alma's place, Ned saw Joplin on the porch. And, out of the tail of his eye, he caught sight of Miss Alma behind a laced curtain. Miss Alma and ol' man Jennings. A pity it still wasn't so. Ned's life was a sight easier when Jennings was alive and making the decisions.

They were barely out of town before the young man said, "Didn't actually meet. We're the Stewart's, suh. I'm Cameron and my sister, hyeh, is Molly."

His condescending tone told Ned that he wasn't being overly polite, just interested in knowing who he was. Ned pushed down his feeling of hostility and reminded himself that these visitors thought they were kin to the owner, and he, just the hired man, which of course, he was.

That wasn't half as hard to push down as the quicksand feeling for the pretty woman at his side. They were so close he could see a tiny mole under her lily-white ear. So close he could smell lavender soap. He tried to shake sister Molly from his mind, but it was something akin to shaking loose flypaper.

"Ned Lawson, foreman of the Rocking J."

Molly turned and smiled the prettiest smile he ever remembered. "Glad to meet you, suh."

Suddenly, like a skittish horse, she turned shy. Ned looked into the distance pretending he hadn't seen the red that raised in her cheeks.

21

"How long ya stayin?" Ned asked, not taking his eye off the path.

Cameron answered. "A month."

A month! Heaven help us. Ned shook his head. Playing nursemaid to these two would cut precious time out of his already long day. Spring roundup to boot. "Only a month! You're going to miss your aunt." He hoped he was the only one hearing the hollowness in his voice. "Word didn't reach her in time. She's out in San Francisco."

He saw the hurt in Molly's eyes. Dirty business this. Made the journey all this way to visit her aunt only to hear she's missed her aunt. The man didn't seem a bit disturbed. Like the Double D baron and his friends, he was probably only interested in hunting wild animals. "Ya plannin' to hunt while you're here?"

"I loath guns and killing for sport." More an accusation than an answer to the question he wished he hadn't asked.

"Not many folks out here kill for sport." Ned hadn't owned a gun himself until Jennings left him his collection. He had nothing against having a gun, just never had the money to buy one. As far as killing for sport was concerned, there wasn't time. "Sometimes Englishmen and Easterners come out to hunt big game. Sorry if I offended you."

"You mustn't think that," the woman quickly said, "he wasn't offended. Were you, Cameron?"

"No, I wasn't offended," he allowed in a monotone.

Seemed a good time to change the subject. "There's a picnic basket if you've a mind to eat." Ned jerked his head to the basket in back just this side of the store-bought supplies.

Cameron kept an eye on the road behind them. "I expect Page is staying in town tonight?"

"Don't rightly know, sir. But you won't be seeing him out this way, his spread's along the Dry Gulch Creek, the Rocking J's along French Creek." Ned thought he felt the woman relax a mite. She must have been mighty tired from the long trip.

Cameron leaned close. "But he said his spread was just over the hill."

Ned heard the braggart, but it was a fairy tale. "Well, reckon it is over a hill. But there's about 4,000 square miles of open range between the two spreads."

Cameron's eyes widened. "Who owns all that land?"

"Government. No reason to file for the land between creeks. Control the water, control the land."

Chapter Five
Molly

Molly had never known such loneliness. She hated this barren, dry land. Why, their so-called French Creek was nothing more than a mud-caked ravine. And she wasn't happy about how the big cowboy hurried them off without even asking if she'd care to visit the facilities at the hotel before they started the last leg of their journey. The hotel was right next to the telegraph office where they stopped. How long would it have taken? More importantly, would her bladder hold out until they reached Aunt Missy's ranch? The land was so empty, no place to hide behind. She'd given anything to see a vine-tangled hickory tree.

Why had she let Cameron talk her into coming? Molly didn't know how much longer she could keep up this facade. She forced back choking tears and told herself to be brave and not give way to her misery. But her shame was powerful.

After nearly a week on the stage listening to mile after mile of friendly talk as they passed through endless nothingness, Molly pretty well had her destiny figured out. She was to be sold to the burly-chested man who talked big to hide his littleness. She was the price to be paid for the family business. She was to be left in this God-forsaken land with that disgusting braggart, never again to see the lush green countryside of home.

She could understand why Cameron was interested in the rich rancher, but she couldn't fathom why Mr. Page had taken to them, poor relations of his neighbor. Maybe pity. Maybe out of loyalty to his friend, Jennings. Maybe she wouldn't have liked her uncle, either. And now the Aunt Missy she'd grown to love and admire from all the stories over the years, the one person capable of saving her from Mr. Page, was off in San Francisco. Why did Aunt Missy have to be gone now?

Molly was jarred from her thoughts as the big driver, she'd forgotten his name, stopped for a bareback rider.

The old plow horse, with a halter in place of a bridle, favored his right front leg. The rider, a boy around eleven, fought for breath. Tears streamed down his face. "Pa's trapped," he said frantically. "Well caved in."

"Yonder?" the driver asked calmly, pointing to a shack on the horizon.

The boy gave a frightened nod.

"Git in back, your horse is played out. He'll find his way home." The man was so calm. Didn't he understand the urgency? Molly wanted to say something to hurry him up, but her tongue was paralyzed. She wanted Cameron to say something to hurry up the man, but he didn't.

The driver understood the urgency after all. The boy was barely in before the man gripped the lines, swung the whip and shot the team ahead. Molly grabbed the plank seat with all her might. A splinter tore through her finger. A shriek caught in her throat.

"What's you name, boy?" the driver hollered over his shoulder.

"Timmy, sir," the boy bravely yelled back.

"Timmy, what?"

"Benton, sir."

"Well, Timmy Benton, we'll see what we can do to help your pa."

"Ma's real sick," the boy burst out, "Pa said she had to stay in bed, but she's not. She told me to fetch the lame horse from the pasture and ride for help."

Molly found her tongue. "And you did just that. Everything will be all right." The driver turned and stared as if to tell her that wasn't the proper thing to say.

The white-knuckled ride ended in the yard of the rundown homestead, the fiery team's lathered sides heaving. Cameron must have swallowed a mountain of dust, the way he was wheezing. He hadn't had an asthma attack in years. And Molly suspected it had more to do with not being in control, than with the whirling dust shrouding them. Before the team had fully stopped, the driver had taken three running steps toward a woman dressed in a shapeless linsey-woolsey, who was frantically clawing at the ground.

Molly jumped out with Timmy. "Hurry, Cameron." Cameron gave his best angry look. "You have to help. The man's trapped!"

"I can't breathe," he said, wheezing.

"Don't start that. You could get Mother's full sympathy and attention by having one of your fraudulent attacks, but not from me." She ran off without listening to his protest of innocence. He was climbing down, however, about the time she got to the well.

"How far down is he?" the driver asked the swollen-bellied woman.

"He was almost finished," cried the woman, a delicate pallor in her thin face.

"Can you free him?" Molly asked before she thought.

The driver shrugged. "Uncurbed wells are always caving in on the digger. Why don't these squatters know better?" he added under his breath. He pointed to the filled bucket and shook his head. He picked up the shovel and motioned to Cameron to come help.

Cameron poked along, wheezing. When he was there, the

driver gave him the shovel and then hurried to the team to free one of the horses.

"How can I help?" Molly asked.

"Here, hold this horse." He hitched it faster than she'd ever seen. "Come here, Timmy." He gave the boy a leg up. "Ride to the Rocking J and tell them Ned said to follow you back. Tell them about your pa and tell 'em to bring ropes, shovels, timber for shoring, and lanterns. Can you remember all that?"

"Yes, sir."

The man named Ned whipped the horse, sending him flying.

Molly followed Ned at a run. Her heart fell as she noticed Cameron leaning against the shovel, staring down at the digging woman. Anger rose in Ned's face as he ripped the shovel out from under her brother. She was angry, too, and ashamed.

"Hey, what the...can't see what the rush is now," Cameron said.

"Reckon you're right, but we won't know 'til we find him." Putting his back into his work, Ned added, "And we won't stop 'til we do."

Cameron deserved the dressing down, even by a servant. She was angry with Cameron over the fat rancher and was rather glad Ned put her brother in his place. What she really liked about this hired man was the way he towered over Cameron, making him look as small on the outside as he was acting on the inside.

But this was no time to worry about Cameron. She put her arms around the woman, who was clearly in the way. "This is man's work. Let's go inside."

"I'm Molly Stewart," Molly said as they started back to the cabin. She wanted to grab the words back the moment they were out of her mouth. It seemed an absurd thing to say to the tortured woman.

"Annie Benton."

Molly was appalled at the one-room cabin. It was dark, shabby, and very small. The kitchen corner boasted a pot-bellied stove with a pipe running out a hole in the roof, a frying pan, coffee pot, and a water pail. Molly led the sobbing woman to the bed halfway hidden behind the flour-sack curtain. The woman was covered with dirt, but the bed was already soiled. She tucked her under the feather tick and then started for the water pail.

A noise from one of the two box crates on top of the two-legged table fastened to the wall caught her attention. It contained the smallest baby she'd ever seen, but the crying was from the other crate. Molly lifted the red-faced screamer and rocked it in her arms as she carried it to the mother. "How old are they?"

"Four days, now." Annie put the baby to breast. "Doesn't seem to help, like old Rosie in the pasture yonder, I don't have milk enough for one." Her dirt-caked hand stroked the baby's head as her fever-dulled eyes looked up at Molly. "Soon they'll be gone, too."

Sadness made Molly turn away. She looked around the cabin deciding what should be done first. The woman had been confined to bed a long time by the looks of the cabin. And from the deep hacking cough, Molly suspected the woman had consumption and would never be better.

The only water she found was in a barrel outside. She helped Annie out of her clothes and cleaned her up the best she could.

Molly was reminded of the *Old Mother Hubbard* rhyme as she cleaned dust from the empty cupboard shelf. Until now, Molly didn't know the meaning of poor.

She slipped the sleeping baby from Annie's arms. "My brother and I are twins. We were as tiny as these hyeh," she said in a feeble attempt at encouragement.

"That's Naomi. The other's Ruth," Annie told her with an air of resignation. Their names only strengthened Molly's resolve. She would do whatever it took to help this woman, just as Ruth maintained her aged mother-in-law by being a gleaner in the fields of Boaz.

Molly whispered, "Entreat me not to leave you or return from following you; for where you go I will go, and where you lodge I will lodge; your people shall be my people, and your God my God; where..." She stopped abruptly as she remember what came next.

Annie finished for her "...where you die I will die, and there will I be buried'." A comforting smile came to Annie's face. "Remembering other people's suffering somehow makes a'body realize how fortunate he is."

Molly tried to think of something to say, but words failed her. She couldn't think of anything this woman had to be thankful for. "Is the rainwater in the barrel outside all you have?"

The woman gave a weak nod.

"Would it be fitting to use a little to boil the diapers?"

Tears welded in the woman's hollow eyes. "That would be too kind of you."

Was that a yes or a no? Hard telling how far they had to haul water, she knew they didn't have a working well. "May I use the water?" Molly asked softly.

The woman nodded as she turned her head into the pillow.

Outside, Molly searched the area around the shack for timber to fuel the fire. What she found was a stack of cow chips. Gingerly she gathered some and placed them under the kettle in the yard. Never would she have imagined herself capable of handling such a thing.

Molly placed the swatches of cloth into the black kettle. The remnants of lye around the sides would have to do. She scraped the flakes and mixed them with the water. Stirring made the splinter from the buckboard dig farther into the skin with each rotation. She reminded herself that her discomfort was nothing compared to the Benton's problems. A faint trace of a green-checked pattern came out in the thin fabric. Annie must have cut them from an old gingham dress.

Shame crept through her as she shaded her eyes and looked into the setting sun to see her brother standing by watching sweat-drenched Ned dig. Her pride in the foreman was as big as her shame in her brother. She'd only known him a short time. Already she had a long list of things she liked about him in addition to an unnamed feeling that tugged at her heart.

Tugging also at her heart was this poor family. How would they survive? The father gone, the mother ailing, two starving babies and a very brave little boy. She would have one of her aunt's milk cows sent over. The least they could do.

Molly went to the buckboard and climbed in. She found the key in her drawstring purse and unlocked her trunk. Rummaging through her clothes, she decided on a white cotton petticoat. Not the most absorbent diaper cloth, but it would do.

Molly spied the gunnysacks of supplies. Coffee, sugar, flour, and salt. They weren't hers to give, but she held fast to the belief that her aunt would do the same thing. Resolutely, Molly returned to the cabin and got out every last container she could find.

After the new diapers were cut and folded, and the babies changed, Molly turned her attention to cooking. She made loaves of sweet bread. Chess pie would have been nice but, running true to this family's luck, the two clucking hens weren't laying.

The light had left the sky before the Rocking J servants arrived. Lanterns were set up around the well as the men worked in shifts to free Mr. Benton or, more likely, bring up his body.

Molly served hot coffee and sweet bread to the tired cowboys who, she understood, had put in a full day already before coming to the homesteader's aid. She was quick to snatch the empty cups, wash them and use them again.

"More coffee?" she asked a lanky redhead, who looked as tired as she felt.

"No, ma'am. You've been too kind already with the lick you've taken with your husband and all. Best if you—"

"Husband? You mean Mr. Benton?" She nodded toward the circle of men shoring up the well. "Mr. Benton isn't my husband. Why I'm—"

"This here's Miss Stewart." Molly all but jumped out of her skin hearing Ned's deep voice behind her. "She and her brother have traveled all the way from Atlanta. Atlanta! Imagine that." There was something in the quality of his voice which puzzled her. Strain? "Bet you don't even know where Atlanta is, O'Malley."

"Sure I do. General Sherman burnt it up during your Civil War."

"War Between the States," Molly said as graciously as bitter feelings allowed. "Yankees may call it a Civil War. Southern ladies and gentlemen remember the atrocities perpetrated by Federalists as the War Between the States."

"O'Malley's an emigrant. The war in the States wouldn't mean a hill of beans to him. Or anyone else out here in the territories."

"It's a pleasure to make your acquaintance, ma'am," the boy said before she had a chance to remind Ned that the West was being settled by Americans, many of whom fought in or lived through the War Between the States. Her aunt, his employer, to name one. Aunt Missy could tell him a thing or two!

"The pleasure's mine, suh. Would you like another?" Molly asked in a sugar-coated tone as she held out the plate of sweet breads.

"Well," he looked around bashfully, "sure. My ma's sweet breads back home don't hold a candle to yours."

"You're just being kind." She thrust the plate toward Ned.

"No, thanks, ma'am." He nodded to little Timmy. "He looks mighty tired."

Poor boy. He looked on, his eyes hooded and his head swaying. She'd become so aggravated she'd forgotten their purpose. "I'll see if I can persuade him to go inside."

"Let me take those for you, ma'am." Ned whisked the plate and coffee pot out of her hands before she had a chance to answer.

She looked over her shoulder to see Ned give the coffee and plate of sweet breads to Cameron. She turned her attention to the poor boy. "Timmy, it's time to go in now."

The boy didn't reply, just looked steadfastly at the well. "Timmy?"

Again Ned was beside her. He took a couple silent steps and swooped the boy up into his arms. Molly matched his long strides with her quicker shorter ones as they headed toward the cabin. She liked the way Ned's dark eyes glistened as he smiled down at the boy. He had a handsome face, but there was more to it than that. Though mean-spirited about the war, he had a gentleness in him.

The boy was too tired to protest when they placed him in his bedding on the dirt floor by the far wall. She tucked the covers around the boy's grimy chin. They were all filthy now. The white boiled shirt Ned had had buttoned to the throat when he met them at the stage was now sweat-slick and missing buttons past his dirt-caked bandanna. The denims that had once gleamed from brushing were dirt-creased. The shining black boots were now dirt brown, and muddy along the worn heels.

"Thank you," Molly whispered.

He squeezed her hand and went out silently.

Molly looked in on Annie. Her eyes were closed but, judging from the coughing and uneven breathing, she was awake. Molly peeked into the crates. Sleeping babies. Quietly she sat down at the table and rested her head against it.

She stirred, feeling a hand on her arm. She must have fallen asleep. She started to say something, but a sweaty hand covered her mouth.

"Shhh," Ned whispered before he took his hand away.

Molly nodded.

He helped her up.

"No, I—"

He put his finger to her lips, silencing her. He blew out the candle and led her to the buckboard.

The lanterns outside threw large shadows of the new men around the well. The worn-out cowboys mounted their horses and headed out in exhausted silence. Molly sat between Cameron and Ned, swaying to the motion of the buckboard traveling along the dark path. "Is there any chance, Ned?"

"There's always a chance until proved to the contrary."

"But there's not much hope?"

His silence was all the answer she needed. Molly searched the star-crowded sky for the North Star and made a wish for the Bentons. She turned to speak to her brother, but all of a sudden felt an overwhelming desire not to hear his voice. Instead she listened to the foreign night sounds. "They need a milk cow."

"I'll see to it in the morning."

"Can't imagine why the woman would choose to stay," Cameron offered.

"Not much choice. Didn't see but that one lame plow horse. The babies and she couldn't make the trip back to wherever they're from even if she wanted to. Most likely, come winter, all but the boy will be planted."

Chapter Six
Page

The sagging buggy sprang up as Page got out. It was a glorious spring day. Everything was going his way. He controlled two of the three big outfits in the valley and now had a chance to bring the Rocking J into the fold. If his plan succeeded, he would control all of the water in the valley. Control the water, control the valley. It gave him a warm, tingling feeling all over.

He glanced up at his four hands, their horses flanking the buggy. They all looked slightly red-eyed this morning and he wondered how much branding they accomplished in his absence. He motioned to the little cabin situated under the shaded cottonwoods bordering Dry Gulch Creek. "Saint, you make sure she's alone." He jerked his head toward the corral filled with cattle. "The rest of you boys check the brands."

Page watched the boys ride out. They were all fine specimen, but favored Saint. Saint had broad shoulders that tapered into a perfect V at the waist, and an arrogant way of walking that told everybody to move aside. Everybody but Page, that is. Saint knew his place where Page was concerned. And watching the proud man kowtow to him made it all that much better.

He scrutinized Saint's dismount and watched him stride

to the shack. Saint took his thumbs from his belt and flexed his hands over his guns as he disappeared through the door. "A gentleman always removes his hat in a lady's home," Page said softly, as if reprimanding his apprentice.

Word had reached Page that the prostitute, Kate, was taking in stolen cattle in trade. It was one thing for a prostitute to sell something that belonged to her, but it was going too far to trade her wares for stolen property. Property that rightfully belonged to him.

Page pulled at the tight fabric around the crotch of his trousers and made a mental note to tell Wong once more to use less starch. The Chinaman understood English only when he wanted to. Page stood at the door and listened. Kate sounded none too happy to see Saint.

"You get out of here, I said."

"There's no call in your being like this," Saint replied.

Page leaned his head around the corner to see what caused the scream. Saint was just giving her a little nudge toward the bed. Her feet flew out from under her and she landed a bit hard against the bedpost. In one swift movement, Saint picked her up and threw her across the bed. It was narrow for a whore's bed and her head struck the log wall. She screamed again. Not overly hospitable to Page's way of thinking.

"I'll give you something to yell about." Saint slapped her hard across the face. He ripped her blouse as she struggled to pull free.

Page decided he'd waited long enough.

"Don't trouble yourself getting up, Kate." Page sat on the edge of her bed and tipped his gray Stetson. "Ma'am." He shook his head as he looked into the woman's frightened eyes. "Cain't teach the boys manners, seems."

The woman clutched her shredded calico blouse, but her generous breasts spilled over all the same. "What do'ya want?"

Page smiled. "Just want to admire you, my dear." He ran a finger up her pink arm light enough to raise gooseflesh. "You're a real beauty." She wasn't. Her features were too small for her round, fleshy face. Though he admired her hourglass bulk. She had wide hips to match her considerable bosom.

She inched away until she had shrunk down against the corner of her headpost.

"You're not afraid of me, are you, my dear?" He reached out and grasped the bare foot in front of him. He massaged it with both hands.

Kate's pale-blue eyes darted from Page to Saint and back again. "What are you fixing to do?"

Page motioned to the door. Saint left. Page smiled at the woman, and then raised her foot to his lips. He nibbled at the toes, tasting the salty sweat. He tightened his grip as she tried to pull her foot away.

"Mister Page?"

He craned his neck around to see Blacky at the door. He was called Blacky because he always dressed in black. Nature had even honored him by coloring his hair and moustache black. Blacky gave a slight nod.

Page turned back to the toes. He licked the ball of her foot until she squirmed and screeched for mercy. He could feel a slight stirring in his loins, but not enough. He bit down on her big toe. Hard enough to taste blood. She screamed at the top of her lungs as she kicked out with the other foot. He caught the offending leg and gave it a cracking twist. "Got my brand in your corral," he hollered above her scream. "Want to know who brung 'em."

Kate tried to scramble from the bed, but Page pressed his weight over her, pinning her down. "I asked you a question!"

She turned her head and buried her face in the moth-worn blanket.

Page tired of smelling the sour sweat that dripped from

the pores of her neck and the grease in her dirty hair. He lumbered up. "Saint, you teach her her manners."

Saint slung his cartridge belt across the oilcloth covering the table and was fumbling at his breeches before Page reached the door. Page looked over his shoulder when he heard the rest of the dress tear away. She had heavy thighs. He liked that in a woman.

One morning Miss Molly had tripped as the horses jostled the stage just as she was descending and he was able to grab her slim thighs to break her fall. He'd forgive her. Owning the Rocking J was much more appealing than heavy thighs.

Page leaned against the log cabin as he looked over all the cattle in the corral. He couldn't understand the mentality of rustlers. His blood boiled thinking of someone trespassing on his land and stealing what was his. Lynching was too good for cattle rustlers. He listened to phlegmy guttural sounds coming from the creaking bed and to the boys cheering Saint on. When the bed was silent and the lesson had been taught, he went back inside. "You didn't have to hurry on my account," he said to Saint's back while the man was buckling his cartridge belt and positioning the holster just so. He paused to give the boys time to finish chuckling at his little joke. "Now, my dear, didn't you have somethin' to tell me?"

Page smiled as the woman tearfully listed her customers.

"And who're you workin' for, my dear?" Page asked in a calm, deliberate manner.

"Tate."

Page didn't know the name. He looked up at Saint. "Tate?"

"Has a cabin down in the Hole-in-the-Wall."

He nodded. "After you boys have your fun with her, string her up." He could hardly stand her screaming, and hurried out.

Page sat in the buggy watching a cloud move slowly over the snow-capped Cloud Peak and poise like a crown atop the rugged Big Horn Mountains. Spring runoff would be starting soon and both creeks would be swollen.

It seemed a long time before the naked woman was dragged to the cottonwood. She fought like a wildcat even after they tied her hands behind her back. Page's eyes were glued to her thighs as she swung from the end of the rope like a pendulum. Back and forth, swaying in the breeze. He pulled at the folds along the crotch of his trousers to relieve the friction of his straining flesh. Timing was everything, he reprimanded himself.

When the mounted boys were beside the buggy, Page threw a bottle up to Saint. Saint uncorked the bottle and gulped down two-fingers worth. Blacky took his share, and then sucked whiskey off the ends of his moustache. Tex and Bill each took a share. Saint siphoned the last few drops with a gargling sound.

Page took the reins in hand. "You boys move the cattle home, then go visit this Tate fellow. I'm going to town." He started to jerk on the reins, then added. "Make sure the slick-eared ones are branded, as well as the Rocking J's."

Chapter Seven
Cameron

Benton, the white-trash homesteader killed in the well cave-in, was buried on Wednesday. Cameron obliged his sister and escorted her to the funeral. A few white-trash families attended, but no one lingered long. The word was out that Mrs. Benton had consumption and no one was particularly interested in coming too close. Except for his fool sister whose heart was so large it blocked her thinking.

He hurried through the house searching for her. "Seen Miss Stewart?" Cameron asked the cook.

The old man grumbled something into his washtub of dirty breakfast dishes.

"I beg your pardon, suh?" Cameron rubbed a rash that had appeared on his neck, probably from dryness.

The fool turned on his game leg and shouted at the top of his lungs. "Try the barn. Didn't hear her ride out yet."

"Thank you so very much," Cameron said sardonically.

Cameron was ready to go home. There was nothing to do in this dry uncivilized land. The people were at best morons. He longed for Southern hospitality where he was entertained in sociable homes by articulate gentlemen and gracious ladies. He missed his weekly game of whisk at the club, and the flirtatious romances with some of the most beautiful women in the world. And as he walked through the spindly grass toward the barn, he realized how much he missed the vibrant flower gardens he'd always taken for granted. He never again would take for granted the serene ocean view from his bedroom terrace, nor the sweet fragrance of gardenias. He scratched the dry, flaky skin on the back of his hands and knew he'd never again complain about the taste of moisture in the air.

He kicked a clod of dirt from the path only to have the specks blow back at him. Granted, it wasn't the gale it had been while on the stage, but it was windy all the same. Not like the gentle breezes off the ocean back home, but squalls that carried the thin prairie dust. He tried to forget his discomfort and concentrate on matters at hand. Daily, Molly had been working from sunup to sundown at the Benton homestead, caring for the widow and the new babies. Now it was Friday, the day of the church social in town, and he had to stop her from going to the Benton place.

She had just finished saddling up when he found her in the barn. He lunged out and pulled her away from the horse. "Not today, you don't."

Molly jerked away. "Leave me alone." The leather creaked and the saddle shifted as she lifted her foot to the stirrup.

The horse circled as he pulled her down. He wiped horse slobber from his sleeve as Molly fumed. "We're going to the box social tonight."

She whirled on him, slits for eyes. "I know what you're plannin' and I don't like it one little bit."

Cameron wasn't sure what she thought she knew. "But you'll do as you're told, ya hyeh? And I say ya don't go the the no-account woman's place today."

"Or what?" came her sassy reply.

Cameron's temper flared, but knowing his purposes were better served with a sprinkling of sugar, he calmly said, "Just be nice to Mr. Page. He's promised to invest in Father's shipping company."

She slapped the end of the reins against the palm of her hand. Her lips were pursed so tightly that the corners of her mouth touched.

He pulled his collar away from the angry rash. "Perhaps we should remember our filial duties. We don't want to see Mama end her days in the poorhouse, now do we?"

Molly bent her head. He had used the right approach; she had a soft spot for every suffering creature, but a blind spot where their mother was concerned. He smiled as she drew the toe of her boot through the hay scattered over the barn floor. "Couldn't we wait the month out? Aunt Missy will be back then." Her eyes were pleading. "Please Cameron, don't make me marry that disgusting fat man."

He backed up. "Marry him? Who said anything about marriage?"

"I'm sure you and Franklin have it all worked out."

"What would make you think such a thing?"

A lamentable laugh escaped her lips. "When were you ever able to keep anything from me? I've known since you decided on the stage. When you told him I made great fried chicken, or whatever it was you said."

Keeping anything from his twin had always been a problem. The other was having to share everything. Though sharing her husband's wealth wouldn't be much of a hardship. He was an old man, after all. How many more years did he have left? "Well, it's done now. He's investing with me."

"But, Cameron, I'll have to stay here. It's so far from Mama and the rest of the family."

"Aunt Missy's here. It must not be so bad if she stayed."

Molly ran her tongue around her lips. It used to be a habit of hers when she was stalling for time to come up with the right answer to those insufferable questions their tutor, Mr. Pendergrass, invariably asked. "But what of my friends?" she stammered.

"You'll make new, better friends."

"But it's so different from home. Everything is so spread out."

"It has its own charm. Miles and miles of open spaces. You'd have to be at sea to feel this vastness."

She sighed. "But Cameron, it's so...colorless. Like the fields after harvest. No, even the barren fields at home have a rich brown soil. This is so...colorless."

"You'll get used to it." He stroked her cheek. "For Mama's sake." He started to walk to the door, then turned back. Molly had buried her face in the neck of the horse and was crying. It hurt to see her like this, but getting back the family business was the most important thing in their lives. Besides, Page was nice enough. She'd grow to like him once she was used to his repulsive appearance. He would probably become even more obese on a steady diet of her cooking. "And speaking of chicken, best be at it."

He backed through the barn door and bumped into Ned and his horse just as he rounded the corner. More horse slobber.

Chapter Eight
Alma

Alma parted the lace curtains to see who was paying a visit. Main Street on the residential side of the creek was much quieter and almost always deserted at this hour. It was Page's buggy.

She would have preferred anyone to Franklin Page. His visits cost her. She had to strike a bargain with Pricilla. She'd get double for going upstairs with him. Seems he wasn't cutting the mustard and was blaming her. Quietly slipping money to Pricilla was better, however, than trouble from him.

Alma watched him brush the trail dust from his gray jacket. With each swipe, the jacket rose to expose the three rolling tiers of his huge stomach that jiggled like jelly. It was a wonder he was even able to get in and out of his buggy, let alone Pricilla.

She let the lace fall and started toward the hall. She stopped in front of the mirror over the mantel and repinned a curl. A cackle from the kitchen assaulted her ears as she descended the stairs. It was early enough in the day that they didn't expect visitors, and she didn't begrudge them their fun, but she wished Laura Jean didn't have such a high-pitched voice.

"Company's comin'," she said as she closed the kitchen door, before she stepped through the gold-fringed red satin curtains onto the foyer's checkered black-and-white marble floor.

"Friday's goin'a be a long one." She heard Dixie say, even through the closed door. More likely a quiet one. The cowboys didn't come to town during roundup.

She opened the door for Page. "Why Franklin, darlin'!" She brushed her lips against his cheek and dabbed her lace handkerchief after to obliterate the red smudge. He stepped over the threshold. "What a pleasant surprise!" She took his kid-gloved hand. "Shall I call Miss Pricilla?"

"You still have *her*?"

Alma gave him her most ingratiating smile. "Now, Franklin, you know me. I couldn't turn out a stray dog. Laura Jean?"

"Just a drink. Ate a peck of dirt on the trail. Saloon's too noisy."

She took his arm. "We'll make it nice and quiet, give you a chance to relax after your long ride."

"Warming up real good, Miss Alma," he said almost child-like as they headed toward the bar. "Spring runoff will be here in no time at all."

"Won't that be just wonderful, Franklin." Spring runoff was everything to the ranchers; to her it meant French Creek would swell up and over its banks and flood her cellar. Joplin and she would be mopping up for weeks. "Just wonderful."

A gentle breeze through the west window twirling the crystal chandelier so that it chimed. Colored sparkles danced across the red velvet wallpaper. She savored the moment, remembering the Venetian showroom filled with bright crystal chandeliers. A rainbow of light had fallen across Jonathan's leathered face, taking ten years off it. She had picked out a smaller one, but Jonathan had insisted on their best. She missed the man so much she ached. Not so much when the house was full of activity and laughter, but during those lonely vulnerable hours when sleep refused to come.

"Please get out a bottle of our finest ambrosia for Mr. Page," she told Joplin. She knew, of course, that he had found a bottle of Page's favorite in the storeroom and had dusted it off even before the man was through the front door. "Let's sit over there." She pointed to the table in the corner where he always sat. She stood beside the chair facing the wall and waited for him to pull the chair out for her. He would sit across from her because he didn't like the vulnerability of having his back to anyone. "Thank you kind suh," she said as he pushed the chair in for her.

Joplin set the bottle and two shot glasses down in front of them. Page threw a double-eagle on the table. Alma picked up the bottle and poured as Joplin scraped the gold coin into his black palm.

"Haven't heard of a big stake poker game tonight," she said in her most playful Southern drawl as he downed his drink. "But can't imagine what else would bring you to town during roundup."

He drew the back of his hand across his wet lips and then belched. "I'm on my way to the box social at the church."

Alma's jaw dropped almost to her lace-covered bosom, and not entirely for effect. A circus elephant performing at a funeral wouldn't be more out of place. "Why Franklin, I declare, you at a church social? A gladiator among the unsuspecting Christians?"

His stomach shook the table as he giggled. He coughed into his chubby fist.

She leaned against the table, her chin cupped in her hand. "Franklin, tell Miss Alma the truth." She spoke to him as if he were a naughty schoolboy. She knew how much he loved being scolded.

He circled the rim of his glass with his finger until the glass hummed. His little-boy eyes looked across the table to her, and then he gave a sheepish smile. "Going to get married, Miss Alma."

"Well, I do declare!" she exclaimed, with what she hoped was just the proper amount of surprise. "And I thought you loved me best." Miss Alma sighed. "Who is this rival of mine? I'll claw her eyes out."

Page looked coyly at her. "You don't know her." He drew a cigar and a one-bladed knife from his breast pocket and whittled at the end. "A young lady." He folded the knife with a click. "From Atlanta." He lit the cigar with a sulfur match and blew a pillow of smoke across the table. "She and her brother are the new owners of the Rocking J," he added, puffing.

Alma's practiced smile froze on her face. The room receded in waves, then circled around her. Her stomach cramped. Anger built as she absently watched him swivel the cigar in his mouth to wet the end. She wanted to run, but instead asked in the most natural voice she could summon, "Ya set a date, yet?"

He poured out whiskey for himself, stopping just short of the rim. "Well, I haven't told her, yet."

Alma clenched her teeth as she looked upon the pompous ass. She never did like the son-of-a-bitch, but his thinking her precious niece would marry the likes of him, made her seethe. "What makes you think she's interested?"

The little boy in him was quick to explain. "Oh, its all settled. Her brother rode out to my spread. It's all agreed. I'm going to invest with him in a shipping business and, in return, Miss Molly's going to be my wife. Goin' to ask her tonight while I'm eatin' her southern fried chicken."

A chilled hand clutched at her heart. Cameron would do that to Molly? Betray his own flesh and blood? She was happy her father hadn't lived to see this day; nothing was more important to him than his family. Of course it was obvious why Page would be interested in the union, since he thought they owned the Rocking J. Almost to herself she said, "And you'll have control of all of the water in the valley."

The boy was no longer there. The fat man laughed his fool head off.

Alma gave a half-hearted laugh. "Well, Franklin," Alma said as she slapped the table and rose to her feet, "Need to get back to my books. Y'all be good, y'hyeh." She gave extra drawl to her words.

She motioned to Joplin as she walked by the bar.

Alma was standing beside the roll-top desk counting the money in the strong box when Joplin knocked. "Come in." She laid out two hundred dollars. "Find Ned and give him this. Tell him to make sure he's the high bidder for Molly's box dinner."

"And if he didn't come to town with her?"

"Give her the opportunity to discover the truth?" Ned was too conscientious for that. Jonathan adored the boy. Said Ned never failed him. Something Alma was counting on.

Joplin shrugged his stooped shoulders, took the money and started out.

The roll-top fell with a sharp thud as she twirled to catch his arm. "Is that enough?"

Joplin pulled a five from the stack and waved it in the air. "This is enough."

She bowed her head. "All the money in the world might not be."

Chapter Nine
Ned

Two boxes sat on the floorboard beside Cameron's feet. One tied with a big yellow ribbon, the other red. Ned lifted Molly from the buckboard, swirled her around and set her down far on the other side of the fresh manure. "You're lighter than a forty-two pound sack of flour."

He noticed a touch of color climb to her cheeks before she turned away. "I'd believe three sacks." She flipped both sides of her cape over her shoulders and fiddled with the dress, which had ridden up. His hands were awkward where women's doodads were concerned. "I shall consider it a supreme compliment, however," she added, without looking his way.

"Thought you said you'd only be a moment," Cameron snapped.

Molly glared up at him. She set her lips as if she were getting ready to say something, but instead twirled around fast enough for her cape to flutter in the wind. It had settled around her ankles by the time she disappeared through the Benton's door.

Ned leaned over the warm-smelling manure and pulled over the box just inside his long reach. He bit his tongue to keep from thanking Cameron for all his generous assistance. A fly lit on the red ribbon. He brushed it toward the other thousand at his feet.

"Hello, Ned," Timmy called, running toward the buckboard.

Ned snatched him up and whirled him high overhead. He put him down and pretended fatigue. "You're too heavy. You must weight as much as three sacks of flour."

The boy beamed with pride. "Red wants to see you." He pointed toward the corner of the shack, like he could see clear through.

"At the well?"

"He's building a corral," he pointed again, "yonder."

"A corral?" The idea of a cowhand building a corral, or any kind of barrier on the open range, went against the grain. He hoped the Rocking J's new owner would never get wind of it. "Tell you what," Ned picked up the box, "you carry this inside for me and I'll go see what O'Malley wants." He placed it in the boy's outstretched hands and tousled his hair.

Ned buttoned his sheepskin jacket against a gust of wind and started off.

"You wanted to see me?" Ned spoke to O'Malley's back.

The hammer flew from O'Malley's hand as nails fell around his feet like spent shells from a trick shootist. He got off a string of evil words while squeezing his thumb between his knees.

"Didn't hear me comin', O'Malley?"

Still crouched, the skinny young man glowered up at Ned.

"Guess not," Ned said behind lips that threatened to break into a grin. "Be black and blue, I reckon."

O'Malley held out his thumb to have a good look. "Reckon so. Hurts like hell. Thank you very kindly for asking."

"Well, if that's all..."

"Wanted to know'd if it pleases you to build a fence to keep the Rocking J's milk cow from strayin'?"

Ned was pleased as punch. He motioned to the nearly finished one behind the kid. "This one?"

O'Malley nodded eagerly.

"Don't hear me telling you to tear it down, do ya?" They stared at each other in knowing silence. Ned turned and started toward the shack. He looked over his shoulder just as O'Malley stuck his thumb into his mouth.

Timmy came whirling around the corner of the shack and bumped off Ned's side.

"Whoa, boy. Where're ya' goin' in such a rush?"

"Red needs my help," he said, without breaking stride.

Ned rapped softly at the door. Even that slight blow threatened to tear the door from its frame. The door creaked open on leather hinges. Molly greeted him with a broom in hand. She lifted a finger to her lips. He tiptoed in as the door creaked closed behind him.

Annie, sitting up in the rocking chair that Ned had brought over from the ranch, rocked one of the babies while her toe rhythmically pressed down on the corner of one of the rocking cradles O'Malley had made. She smiled up at Ned with the same fear of speaking. No one wanted to wake the babies. Her face was pasty white and her sunken eyes were laudanum glazed. The ivory lace shawl around her frail shoulders looked mighty fancy for the poor squatter's widow, and Ned suspected it was Molly's.

Molly leaned the broom against the table and picked up the red-ribboned box. She handed it to Ned. "The other one," she whispered as she turned him around and pushed him toward the door. The door creaked as he left.

Cameron had spent his time braiding the ends of the reins, to the annoyance of the team, judging from the distance they had moved.

"Could you push that box over here?" Ned asked as he placed his box on the floorboard.

Cameron clawed his collar as he prodded the box with his foot, and then gave it an all-out kick. "Tell her if she isn't out in one minute, I'm coming in after her."

"Yes, sir." Ned surveyed the damages to the box as he headed to where he could see O'Malley. "O'Malley," he called out at a distance. Both O'Malley and Timmy turned. "Put some grease on the door hinges before you drive another nail into that thing." Ned popped out the dent in the side of the box.

O'Malley nodded, or scratched his head. Ned wasn't sure which.

Ned winced and tiptoed across the floor in sync with the squeaking door. He placed the box on the table. He caught Molly's eye and thumbed toward the door.

Molly took off the tattered apron and exchanged it for the cape over the back of a table chair. She whispered that she'd be back tomorrow as she threw on the cape, then side-stepped around Ned.

Ned gave Annie a quick tilt of his hat and managed to sweep through the door behind Molly on the same grating creak. Molly wavered as a wail rose from inside, but Ned took her elbow and nudged her forward. The ice-blue stare from her brother hurried her along.

They rode silently to town. Molly kept looking over her shoulder. Cameron stared into the horizon, rubbing his neck. And Ned focused his eyes on the road ahead, trying to come up with a plan for the here and now.

Molly spoke as the town came into sight. "Please be so kind as to leave me at the general store, suh. I'll walk the rest of the way."

Ned needed to pick up a few supplies for Shorty, but he'd wait until morning lest they disappear off the buckboard over night. He was just figuring to tell Molly when Cameron cleared his throat to speak.

"Do you need to purchase something, Molly dear?" Cameron asked with great concern. Ned couldn't figure it. Cameron would marry his sister to the likes of Page when he knew full well she didn't want to be hitched to him, and yet he seemed so concerned about her needs.

"The babies are in need of diaper cloth. Something more absorbent than what they're using now."

Cameron didn't acknowledge. He seemed miffed, if Ned could go by the way he crossed his legs, folded his arms and threw back his head to look at the landscape.

"Shall I take you over to the church first, Cameron, then bring back Miss Stewart to help her with the packages?"

Cameron turned and sneered, but spoke in his customary soft drawl. "I'm in no hurry. We'll all purchase diaper cloth."

Ned drew rein in front of Tulley's General Store. He tied off as Cameron helped Molly down. The bell over the door jingled and the proprietor looked up from taking an inventory of stock to give Molly a smile. Cameron didn't follow her in, instead he looked the town over. Ned leaned against a water trough, soaking up the warming sun and fumbling in his pocket for tobacco. He watched Molly's brother cross the street, sweeping clear of a fresh pile of horse-droppings. When he disappeared behind the bat-winged doors, Ned pocketed the tobacco bag. He rushed along the boardwalk to the end of the street, crossed over to the narrow alley up the next street and forded French Creek over the little foot bridge. He entered Miss Alma's through the back door.

"Beg your pardon, ladies." Ned tipped his hat. The four flimsily clad girls sitting around the kitchen table returned noble nods. "Through here?" He walked toward the doors.

"If you desire to be somewhere other than in here." It was Laura Jean's voice. He knew it, even though he had his back to the girls and was out the door. Her voice could shatter a beer mug.

He spread the gold-fringed, red satin curtains and ducked through. It was dim in the house, especially after hours in the bright sunlight, but not too dark to see Page sitting at the corner table in the bar. Page was relighting the stub of a cigar and didn't seem to notice him. Ned backtracked. The slightest whispering of the floorboards under carpeted padding roared through his ears like a speeding train. The swishing curtains seemed to clang out like a mission bell, and the slowly turning doorknob clicked like the report of a buffalo gun. He slipped through the door, closed it softly, and leaned against it.

"What's wrong, Ned?" Dixie asked. "You look like you've seen a—"

Ned put his finger to his lips, stopping her. All four girls were wide-eyed with wonder, but not even Laura Jean spoke.

"Dixie, would you go with me upstairs?" Ned whispered. "Real quiet like."

She looked around the table at the other girls. "You don't want Miss Alma to know you're here?" she whispered back.

"Don't want Page to know."

"Page here?" Pricilla asked with a groan.

He pointed in the direction of the bar.

Dixie twirled the nearest lock of hair around her finger as she thought. She shrugged, stuffed the rest of the banana in her mouth, and then started toward him.

As they entered Page's viewing range, Ned stooped way over and buried his face in her curls. He turned just enough to see Page before Dixie and he started up the stairs arm-in-arm. Page didn't seem to notice him and, if he had, he wouldn't have thought much of it now that Dixie was on his arm.

Dixie was fumbling with his belt buckle before he'd gotten the door closed. Ned mislead her as to his intentions with his pawing on the stairs. "Dixie," he said, pushing her to arm's length, "it's Miss Alma I came to see." He turned her loose and fixed his buckle.

"Miss Alma doesn't come upstairs with the customers." Her voice was indignant. The girls worshipped the ground

Miss Alma walked upon and he had come dangerously close to insulting her.

"No, I didn't mean…I need to see her. She'll want to hear what I've come to say." He ran a finger along the soft, warm folds of her neck. "Please fetch her up."

"Since you asked so nice, Ned honey," she said, sashaying out.

Ned felt a little foolish being in the upstairs room alone. He'd never noticed the decor before. It was gaudy now that he was having a good look. There was a picture over the bed of naked plump lady lounging on a big lily-pad in a pond. She was downright ugly. Miss Alma must have bought the picture to show what queen-bees her girls were. The wallpaper was three-dimensional. Anyhow, the red was. It was kind of velvet-like hearts and curly-Q's pasted on white satin.

Ned took off his hat when he heard the door open. Miss Alma, dressed in a red satin dress that matched the red on the walls, lifted her skirts above trim ankles as she came through the door. She settled her skirts before closing the door behind her.

"I'm glad you came, Ned. Did Joplin find you?"

"He's looking for me?"

"Yes, I needed to see you. First, though, I want to thank you properly for helping me. I know you consider it a big risk."

Ned covered his forehead with his arm. It was the only untanned part of his face, and he didn't want her to see him blush. "It was nothing, ma'am."

Miss Alma walked to the window and looked down on Main Street. "Page plans to marry Molly."

"But that's what I'm comin' about. Cameron's planning to marry her off, all right. And Molly isn't happy about it."

"Franklin's planning to ask her at the box social. So the first thing we have to do is see to it that he doesn't get the chance."

Ned nodded, though he didn't know how they could keep Page from doing what he intended to do.

"I gave Joplin two hundred dollars to give to you. I want you to buy her box dinner. If it costs more than that, I'll give you more."

Two hundred dollars! That was a good four months pay! He swallowed hard thinking about paying that much money for a box dinner.

"I can't imagine Franklin topping that." Miss Alma paced the floor. "I'm sending a letter to my sister Beatrice...the twins' mother...tellin' her I want to invest some money in her deceased husband's shipping concern. With any luck, she'll telegram Cameron before it's too late."

Ned scratched his head. Her kind of business was a mite more lucrative than he suspected. But then anyone willing to pay two hundred dollars for a box dinner had to have money.

Miss Alma was at the door. "You wait hyeh a few minutes in case Joplin's back. I'll send him up if he is, otherwise you look around town for him."

Ned didn't have a chance to tell her that Miss Molly and her brother had to be sitting in the buckboard fuming as it was.

Miss Alma came back in and closed the door behind her. "I heard Molly's been helping the squatter family that had that well accident. It made me proud, somehow."

"You can be a sight more proud. She's a fine girl."

Miss Alma gave him a knowing smile. What she knew, he had no idea, but it made him very uneasy.

Chapter Ten
Ned

Ned touched the bulge in his britches. Two hundred dollars of someone else's money could make a man mighty uncomfortable. He'd checked the pocket twice for holes before he tucked the bills in.

Page and Cameron stood under a cottonwood on the other side of the sloping church ground. Wanting to be as far away as possible, Ned positioned himself on the outside of the last knot of men, and would have followed a group of running boys down to the banks of French Creek if he hadn't feared missing the auction. Molly stood a foot taller than the other young ladies lined up against the church's white-washed wall behind the long table of gaily wrapped boxes. She looked forlornly toward the Big Horn Mountains. The girls on either side were turned to their neighbors, leaving no one for her to chat with.

The preacher broke from a group of married women and started toward the table. He raced in under the circling skip rope and managed to jump three times to the delight of his partner and the two girls at each end of the rope. He untangled the rope from his feet and hurried toward the table, all the time cackling with the folks. He moved down the line of young ladies, chatting to each girl and offering his hand to Molly. When he stood to the side of the table, a hush came over the crowd.

One by one the boxes were sold. Two dollars seemed the expected price. Ned almost bid on the last one, which went for two bits more than the first three. It gnawed at him knowing that one of the girls was going to share her box dinner with Cameron.

Ned felt the bulge again with his sweaty palm. The preacher held up the box with the red ribbon. Ned looked across the crowd to where Cameron and Page were standing. Cameron whispered in Page's ear. Page nodded, the lit end of his cigar dancing like a firefly.

The preacher cleared his throat with a sluggish gurgle. "What do I hear bid for this lovely box with the red ribbon?"

Page tucked a thumb under each lapel. "Five dollars," he shouted around the cigar.

A murmur of gasps floated above the crowd. Heads turned toward the bidder.

Ned tried to speak but nothing came.

"Going once, going—"

"Ten."

Heads turned in Ned's direction. He reminded himself what would happen if he didn't win the bidding.

The preacher shifted the box to one hand in order to shade his eyes against the slanting sun with the other. "Did I hear ten?"

"Fifteen," Page called, blood coming to his face.

The preacher looked at the box in hand. He turned and looked at the ladies as if asking what was in it. No one admitted ownership. He turned back, remembering his purpose. "Do I hear twenty?"

"Twenty," Ned repeated loudly, so as to hear himself over his pounding heart and banging knees. Everyone was gawking at him like he was a damned fool.

"Fifty." Page's voice was angry and his glare was deadly.

The preacher's face turned heavenward. Molly's turned

toward Ned, but by no stretch of the imagination did hers look angelic.

"Seventy-five." Ned wiped the beads of perspiration from his face.

"One hundred!" Page shouted hoarsely.

Ned's eyes darted to Molly. She was staring daggers.

"Two hundred." Ned's ears heard what his mind thought. Two hundred dollars of a working woman's money! He closed his eyes waiting for Page. Ned decided right then and there that would be his last bid no matter what Miss Alma had said. He didn't hear Page's bid over the roar of the crowd. He opened his eyes and looked beyond the blur of faces. Only Cameron stood under the tree. Page was storming toward his buggy.

"Sold."

Ned's legs threatened to collapse. *Two hundred dollars!* He stood as if paralysed.

The preacher didn't wait for the formality of the high bidder bringing up the money. Guarding the box with his life, he rushed toward Ned. The crowd parted like the Red Sea and the preacher was standing before Ned.

Ned dug in his pocket and placed the wad of bills in the holy man's outstretched hand.

The preacher delivered the box. "We'll have our pipe-organ a sight sooner thanks to your kind generosity, Brother."

Ned was twixed. Credit wasn't due him, but he didn't think Miss Alma would want her name brought up. Too, the good Christians of French Creek might not take kindly to having a good portion of their organ bought by the madam of the local whorehouse. "I'm sure it's a good cause."

The preacher walked slowly back, counting all the way.

People had to be coaxed to bid on the last two boxes. Both went for ten dollars, but after Ned's bid, ten was anticlimactic.

Molly walked briskly toward him when the auction closed.

She passed him and kept right on walking all the way down the slope to the bank of French Creek. Ned wasn't so sure she didn't intend to walk through it, but she plopped herself down on a boulder at the water's edge. She fidgeted with the pearl button on her glove.

He sat cross-legged, Indian-style, on the dirt beside the boulder and set the box between them.

Ignoring him, Molly scooped up a handful of pebbles and tossed them one at a time into the water. Ned picked up a flat one and skipped it to the other side.

Molly glanced over. "Let's see if you can do that again." She seemed amused as he skipped another, not once but twice. "Try it again," she said, swatting at the swarm of circling mosquitoes.

"Here, stand up." He placed a pebble in her hand, then covered the back of it with his. "Now flip your wrist," he said, showing her. The pebble skipped once and almost made it across to the other side. Molly smiled in spite of herself. She tried it alone, but it sunk.

"Try again."

Her next one skipped. She jumped up and down. Then, as if remembering about the box dinner, she returned to the boulder.

Ned sat down and turned his attention to the box. He untied the ribbon, spread out the red-and-white checked tablecloth, and placed the white frosted cake on it. Following that, he brought out the sourdough biscuits, and then the plate of golden fried chicken.

His mouth watered as he held up the plate to offer Molly a piece. Molly shook her head and skipped another pebble. "Sure?"

She ignored him.

Ned took a big bite of the plump leg. He chewed twice before the fire engulfed his mouth. He looked up at her. She was biting down on her ruby lips. Ned swallowed hard.

Molly tossed another pebble. "Worth two hundred dollars, Ned?"

"Might have a tad much pepper," he said, getting to his knees and stretching over the slow-moving water, his cupped hands scooping up the cold liquid as fast as he could slurp it.

"Page looked the type to like peppery things."

He dove prone, supporting himself with his hands and lapped water against the burning tongue. Only slightly did he feel the water breaking around his wrists. The dull pain from the sharp hidden rock under his right palm became more intense as his mouth cooled. He pushed up and returned to the spunky woman's side.

The sleeves of his jacket were wet almost to his elbow. Ned rubbed his freezing hands together with a rasping sound to stimulate circulation. "Will I like the cake?"

Molly skipped another pebble. "Might be a tad salty for *your* taste." She chanced a quick glance at him. "Page somehow looked like a salty ol' boy, thought *he'd* like it."

They laughed.

"It's getting dark." Molly rose. "You come by the house tomorrow evening and I'll see if I can do better." She extended her hand. "Now, come on, I'll buy you dinner at the hotel."

Ned put everything back in the box. "That's a deal."

She slipped her hand through the crook of his arm as they walked back up the slope.

"Know now why you were so set on leaving the yellow-ribboned box at the Benton's."

She threw back her head and laughed. She was as beautiful as she was feisty.

They passed several twosomes eating box dinners as well as the married folk and children at the church social, who were enjoying the carry-in feast. Ned tipped his hat at a group of gawking women.

"Reckon they think me an all-fired fool," he said when they were well out of hearing distance.

"I think you're an all-fired fool." She shook her head. "Two hundred dollars."

The knot in his stomach tightened like a noose around a condemned man's neck. He wished he could tell her the truth. "Well, it was for a good cause. Every church should have a pipe-organ."

Chapter Eleven
Cameron

The Egyptian Saloon was quiet and orderly, unlike the dime-novel accounts Cameron had stocked up on before making the journey out west.

A painting over the bar depicted a pyramid, and a crooked frame of a camel was hung along the side wall in a futile attempt to hide a diagonal crack. The frontier bar failed pathetically in its Egyptian motif.

"What'a ya 'ave?" the burly, barrel-chested bartender asked in a deep bass voice, stroking his long grizzly beard.

"A beer," Cameron replied.

The bartender hooked a filthy mug around a hairy knuckle and pulled on the white china handle.

"A bottle."

The mug wobbled as it landed. "A bottle," the bear-like bartender repeated as unenthusiastically as a schoolboy reciting a poem. He ducked out of Cameron's sight and came back up, blowing on a dusty quart bottle. He gave it another blow for good measure after the top was opened, sending a torrent of spittle and the remaining specks of dust down the opening. The bartender sat it in front of him with a thud. "Eight bits."

A dollar for a beer was outrageous. A dollar for one with spit floating on the surface was an abomination. He slapped a silver dollar on the wet bar. The man swept it into his paw.

Cameron picked up the precious quart bottle and threaded through the quiet room toward a table in the corner near the piano. Not that he was overly enthralled with the talent of the player, but he wanted to join the distraught Page. It was Page or the only other patron of the bar. The way the other man shuffled cards gave Cameron a notion of his profession, and he thought joining him might cost more than the beer. Besides, his needs were better served calming Page.

"May I join you, suh?"

Page poured out another and tossed it down. Cameron pretended to be interested in the moving piano keys, all the time debating whether or not to repeat the question. Page cleared this throat. "Suit yourself."

Not the most gracious invitation he had ever received, but it would suffice. He pulled out the chair across from Page, careful to avoid hitting the piano player's stool. He fortified himself with a couple of pulls on the quart bottle and pondered how to begin. He measured his words. "Did you see how unhappy Molly looked that you didn't get to share her fried chicken?"

"No?"

Cameron nodded. "Yes."

Page took out a cigar and sliced through the tip with his one-blade knife. As he struck a match, Cameron slipped a nearly new cigar from the ashtray and crushed it underfoot.

"Remember how anxious she was for me to make sure you knew it was the red-ribboned box?" Cameron fanned the air to chase away the rotten-egg smell of the sulfur match.

"That's right!" he exclaimed, between puffs. "Poor thing havin' to eat with a hand." His bloodshot eyes were ablaze with concern. "I'll have to do something to make it up to her." He twirled the cigar in his mouth, wetting it. "What do ya think she'd like?"

Cameron was quite sure nothing Page gave her would be

appreciated. "Maybe a ring?" Cameron knew that would go over in a big way with her. Probably shove it down his throat.

The table shook under Page's fist. "Yes! A big, big diamond. The biggest in the territory!"

Too big to swallow, Cameron hoped.

"Play some of that new-fangled music you was a'playin' the last time, Sam." Page popped the piano player hard enough on his back to cause the man's hands to hit a sour chord.

Page seemed on top of the world now. He rose and pranced in time with the snappy tune over to the gambler.

As they started drawing for high card, Cameron took up a station behind his big benefactor. It became quite obvious to Cameron that it was no place for amateurs, or a man uneasy with the idea of losing a big wad of money. Page was losing heavily. He probably figured losing money at the table would make up for not bidding over two hundred, which is what he should have done. It made Cameron uneasy about the investment, wondering if maybe Page was a bit tight-fisted. Page losing with good humor would have relieved Cameron.

The gambler wore a black suit, a tad shiny in the elbows, and a crisp ruffled shirt boiled white, frayed at the cuffs. He let Page win every fourth cut or so. Just enough to leave Page wanting more. A little smile twitched his thin waxed moustache each time Page won.

Page lorded winning over the gambler. But it wasn't so. Page doubled his bet each time he won, only to lose. The gambler would be leaving with much more in his pocket than he came in with, and Page less.

As the night wore on, more and more people crowded in. The big green gambling table was elbow-to-elbow. The noise level ebbed and flowed.

"My lucky night," Page said as he raked in the chips.

The gambler restacked the chips Page sideswiped. For the

last few hands, the gambler had done little more than ante. The others were losing heavily to Page.

"Sure is." The gambler shuffled the deck.

Page handed the empty whiskey bottle over his shoulder. Cameron dutifully replaced it with a full one and two fairly clean glasses. Cameron wiped his out with a handkerchief before pouring drinks.

The stinking smoke hung in the still air, watering Cameron's eyes. A sudden giddiness from the liquor made him consider joining the game when the storekeeper at Page's right cashed in, but he hesitated too long and the undertaker slipped in. It was just as well. The shipping concern was far too important a venture to risk losing Page's support by beating him at cards. Nor did Cameron want to lose his traveling money to secure that support. Leaving Molly in the territories was enough. He felt a tug of pity for her, but pushed it out of his mind. He was resolved. The family business had to be regained, no matter what the sacrifice.

Page clicked the chips as he made up his mind whether to raise or call the only player left in the hand, the gambler. He tossed out ten chips. "I'll see your raise and..." He pushed out a stack. "...raise you fifty."

The gambler folded.

Page revealed his hand, not that he needed to, he probably just wanted everyone to have a good look at all the pictures. "Three ladies and two gents." Page took the cigar out of his mouth and rolled the wet end between his tobacco-stained fingers. "Ever seen prettier ladies?" He stuck the cigar between his teeth as he raked in the pot.

The gambler put a hand on Page's cards just as the next dealer started to pick them up. His mask was gone, replaced by a vermillion flush. "This is how you play poker?" He picked up his folded hand.

"Are you calling me a cheat?" Page's hidden hand swept above the table, a fully-cocked Colt's Derringer drawn.

The gambler placed his cards face down on top of Page's. He tossed off his drink, and then picked up his chips. "Got a long stagecoach ride tomorrow." He rose. "Time to cash in and call it a night."

Page eyed him with uncertainty. When the gambler was gone, Page eased the dinky pistol off cock and under the table, presumably to wherever he kept it on his person. He puffed out his chest. "We can spread out a bit now, boys, and play a friendly game."

Chapter Twelve
Ned

Ned woke from a sound sleep to the commotion on the hotel's stairs. As his mind cleared of cobwebs, he recognized the voices of the drunken twosome, Cameron and Page. He had gone looking for Cameron after seeing Molly to her room following a pleasant dinner and a promise that the fried chicken dinner tomorrow night at the ranch would top even that. He didn't care all that much what her cooking was like, he just enjoyed being around her. Enjoyed her company a lot better than her brother's.

He found her brother at the saloon. Ned stayed long enough to see that the boy was keeping out of trouble. There was one tense moment when Jim Talbot, the gambler from Deadwood, started to challenge Page's three queens. And no wonder. When Jim picked up his hand, Ned saw it over his shoulder. He had a fourth queen, but three of them were black.

Hearing a thud, Ned got out of bed and jumped into his pants, then tugged at his boots. His head was clear now, and he suspected that the other guests in the hotel were most likely awake.

Cameron was sprawled out on the landing next to Page, both giggling like schoolgirls. Ned stuck Cameron's hat firmly on the boy's head, and then threw him over his shoulder.

"You!"

Ned craned his neck to see Page. The man was on his knees, a finger pointed at him. Page collapsed, his chin scraping the edge of the banister. As far as Ned was concerned, Page could bed down where he was, but Cameron was his responsibility. He shifted the boy's weight.

"You horseshit cowboy," Cameron said, hungry for revenge. "Who gave you leave...you stupid son-of-a-bitch. I know what you are trying to do."

Ned carried Cameron up the next six steps and down the hall to his room. "If it is your intention to wake everyone in this hotel, then you are doing a dandy job of it." He flopped him on the bed like a ragdoll. The springs squeaked as the bed bounced, then sagged with a slow sigh. His hat fell off and rolled across the threadbare carpet.

"My hat." He tried to lift a hand to his head. "My arm. My arm is missing."

"It's in your sleeve. I'm taking off your coat."

Futilely, Cameron threw punches with trapped arms.

"Settle down and it will go better for both of us."

Cameron got off a string of raw words, his genial soft drawl no longer in evidence, as Ned struggled with his dandy boots.

"This sock goes in your mouth with the next word you utter."

"You will never—"

Cameron gagged and turned blue. Convulsed. Ned jerked the sock out of his mouth, vomit followed like lava from an exploding volcano. The stench rose far faster. He lifted Cameron to a sitting position, lest his charge choke to death.

Ned grabbed for the washbasin. The white crackled-glazed pitcher wobbled, splashing cold water across Ned's hand, as the basin skidded along the top of the maple dresser. He steadied the pitcher on the dresser while he shoved the basin under Cameron's chin. The second wave of liquor-vomit splattered into the basin. Ned's stomach pitched and threatened to join in. He turned away, gagging.

Cameron fell back, out cold.

Ned fumbled with the vomit-slick studs, and then peeled the soaking wet shirt off of Cameron's chest. He poured water over the towel, worked up a paltry lather from the fresh bar of soap, and cleaned Cameron as best he could. And left him.

He slipped out only to be greeted by Page, hunkering down against the bannister.

"I'm going to get you for the damage you done me," Page said, his voice shrill.

Ned looked at the stinking drunk old shoat. Deciding he wasn't worth the breath it took to speak, he turned away and headed to his room.

"You come back here, I'm not finished, you thieving bastard." Page stumbled toward him.

"Mr. Page, go to bed. You're wakin' everybody up."

"This is *my* country. I damn near own everything and I'll do as I damn well please." Page fell against the paper-thin wall, flickering the gas lamp overhead.

Molly came out of her room, pulling a robe over her chemise. She padded down the hall on lily-white toes. "Let me help you to your room, Mr. Page." She put her arms around him.

Ned's eyes burned with a lambent flame as he watched Page run his pudgy fingers through the folds of her robe.

"Here, I'll do it." Ned pulled the lump of lard to his feet, getting a good whiff of him in the bargain.

"Miss Molly, did I wake you?" Page asked like a naughty child pleading forgiveness from his mother.

Molly propped herself under his other arm. "Come on, it's late. We'll help you to your room." The key fell from his hand as he buried his face in her neck.

Ned bent over to have a look. "Number three."

They looked around and came to the same conclusion.

"Behind us."

"On the landing."

It took the whole width of the hall to turn around. Ned gave the key a kick, propelling it down the hall. It jingled to a stop against the pane of the window on the landing.

They hesitated at the top of the stairs. Page took the deciding step, Molly and Ned tumbling after. Page cushioned their fall. Ned felt soft warm flesh against his bare chest. He jerked back, covering Molly's milky-white leg with her robe. With the image of her trim ankle and well-defined calf engraved solidly on the walls of his mind, he scrambled to his feet and lifted Molly to hers. He ran a hand along the dusty windowsill until he found the key. He unlocked the door to the suite, all the time aware of Page pawing Molly.

The threesome stumbled through the well-appointed room, toward the bedroom. "Turn down the spread, I have him." Molly hurried ahead as Ned and Page squeezed through the door. They fell together on the bed, sending the mattress through the slats with a sudden snap.

Page threw his arm around Ned and nuzzled against his ear. "Will you marry me?" he mumbled.

Ned struggled out from under him and climbed out of the crater.

"We can't just leave him like this," Molly whispered.

Ned couldn't see why not, but he tugged at a boot until a stockinged foot fell out of it. Same with the other foot. Molly twisted and yanked at Page's coat. Ned climbed over the iron railing and crawled along the edges of the mattress to give her a hand. He was rewarded with a glancing blow, a nine of spades and a three of hearts. Ned let go of Page's arm. "He's good."

"We should—"

"Leave him." He supported Molly's velvet-sleeved elbow as he escorted her from the room.

At her door, Molly turned to Ned. She seemed shorter somehow, and vulnerable. Her cheeks flushed, and she pulled her robe together at the neck. For the first time Ned realized he was bare-chested. He held his arm against the ringlets of black chest hair in an ineffective attempt at covering himself.

"Goodnight," she whispered.

"Goodnight," he whispered back. It was then he realized what was different about her. Her golden hair cascaded in one thick sleek mane down her back instead of the usual curls piled high on her head. "You're one beautiful woman, Molly Stewart. All the way through."

Her eyes fell to her bare toes as she stepped back inside her room and closed the door.

He leaned up against the wall for a moment to breathe in the night's cool air. Lightly he stepped along the creaking floorboards to his room.

Chapter Thirteen
Saint

Tate's shanty cabin was located close enough to the red cliffs on the east side of the Middle Fork in the Hole-in-the-Wall to be shaded from the morning sun. Saint, Blacky, Tex and Bill stopped at the edge of the timber and fanned out. Saint looked past the babbling creek to the open meadow fronting the cabin, trying to figure out the best approach. Three white-tails at the creek's bank snapped to attention at the horses' whinnying.

Saint motioned to Tex. Tex clicked his mount ahead. The deer scattered and were out of sight before Tex struck water. He was shot for his effort. The horse reared up at the rifle report, throwing Tex off with a hollow splash, hooves slipping and scrambling for solid footing. Tex's limp body was trampled and finally trapped under the fallen horse. It screamed, and kicked, and finally managed to right itself. The horse bolted up the near bank toward the evergreens, in total disregard for the welfare of its rider. Bill took out after it.

"The rest of you, git," the voice in the shadowy cabin yelled.

Saint rose in his stirrups. "Tate, that you?"

"Who wants to know?"

"Don't know that we rightly met. Peters's the name."

"Peters, you and your boys are trespassing," Tate hollered. "Now git."

"You had no call to kill him. We just came to talk."

"Is that a fact?" The voice was flat with disbelief.

Saint glanced at Blacky for inspiration. Blacky tugged on his somber-curved moustache. "Sent to tell you something."

"Who sent you?"

"Kate."

"Is that a fact?"

Saint could tell he wasn't taking bait. "She had some trouble with squatters. Wants you to come right away."

"Take you all to fetch the message here?"

"We was heading to the fort. Told Kate we would take her message seeings how it weren't all that far out of the way."

Saint slouched back, his spine against the cantle, and waited. And waited.

Leather creaked as Blacky threw his leg over the pommel. "Been thinkin' on your words mighty long, Saint."

Saint cut his eyes to Blacky. "Reckon what we should do about it?"

Blacky shrugged. Bill rode up on the other side of Blacky, leading Tex's spooked horse.

"Did you git a good look at Tex?"

Bill shook his head.

"Floating face down is good as dead," Blacky reasoned.

Their interlude ended with Tate's words. "Did she send something of hers as proof?"

Saint leaned over the pommel and looked beyond Blacky to quiet Bill. "Look if Tex still gots that lucky hanky from his Mexican whore down El Paso way?"

Bill swung down and rifled through Tex's water-spurting saddle bag. He handed the lacy hanky up to Blacky. Blacky pinched a corner between his leather gloves and trailed it across his horse's neck to Saint.

Saint waved him off. He rose up to call to Tate. "Her hanky. Said you know'd the one."

Blacky retraced his course. He waited for Bill to remount. "He don't want it."

"I don't want it neither."

"Take it anyhow." Blacky flicked his fingers and the hanky floated between them. Bill swooped it up stirrup level.

"Want to see it," Tate hollered.

Saint waved Bill ahead.

A sheet of red masked his ashen face. "He'll shoot me like he did Tex."

Bill was believed in some company to be dull-witted. Saint reevaluated this belief.

Blacky pulled the water-spotted reins out of Bill's hand. "Never know'd such a crybaby." He slapped Bill's horse on the rump. Bill reeled back as his horse dashed through the trees. He recovered sufficiently to hold the hanky well overhead as his spirited horse charged over the bank and plummeted into the water. A shot rang out midstream. Bill staggered, clutched at his chest, and gasped long enough for Saint to cringe. The horse pranced and side-stepped against the confusing signals of the bridle holder. Bill toppled as the horse climbed the far bank.

Those few seconds stretched into an hour as Saint looked on helplessly.

"Kate never owned a hanky her whole life," Tate yelled. "Now, who sent you?"

"Can't believe that," Blacky mumbled. "Every sniveling child has some kind of hanky."

Saint eyed Blacky with contempt, and then turned back to the cabin. He rose in his stirrups. "Page sent us, you thieving cattle thief. Already strung up your whore. Pity. None better."

Bullets whistled through the trees. A lucky one hit Blacky square through his gloved hand. Bill wasn't the crybaby by

74

the sound of Blacky's yelping and carrying on. He jumped from his horse and gnawed his glove like a trapped wolf chewing off its own paw. Saint dismounted and ground-reined his horse. He gave Blacky's flesh wound a perfunctory glance, stripped off his kerchief and tightened it around the bloodied hand.

"Now what?" Blacky asked after some serious silence, save his own moaning and groaning. He cradled his wounded hand.

"Wait for Tate to make his move."

The sun climbed high in the sky and blazed down through the tops of the trees. Evergreens grew straight and narrow in the Hole-in-the-Wall, and provided little shade. Saint adjusted his coat-pillow under his head and looked wistfully at the gurgling creek.

"Gettin' mighty thirsty." Blacky was stretched out under the neighboring tree, seething with extra care every time Saint looked his way.

"Own fault. No one said you had to wear black."

"Not thirsty?" Blacky uncrossed his boots, and then recrossed them the other way.

"I can stand it."

"Stand it longer in a cool cabin, bet'ya. Might never make his move. Maybe we should make his move for him."

"How's that?"

"Been chewing on a plan."

"And?"

"Burn him out. The way I cipher it, can't get much hotter."

"That's a right smart plan. You do just that."

He held out the wrapped hand. "Reckon you should do it. I'll cover you." His left hand crossed his body and pulled the Colts out of the holster backwards. He flipped it in the air to right it.

Saint gave it some thought. After weighing this solution against spending even more time listening to Blacky moan, against his thirst, and against Page's wrath at one cattle thief hiding behind a rifle, he favored the plan.

He made a wide swing around the cabin, wide enough to keep from drawing gunfire. Procuring timber to blaze wasn't as easy as it looked, not with someone shooting through chinks between the logs. He scratched together wet pine needles and cones at the back cornerstone, dodging first one way, then the other. The pile smoldered for what seemed an eternity before it ignited into a glorious conflagration. He hadn't quite crossed the creek before he heard the door burst open. He looked downstream to see Tate running toward the creek, peppering the timber with slugs.

Blacky returned fire with a vengeance, emptying his revolver into the cattle thief.

Chapter Fourteen
Ned

Ned picked up the rig at the livery while Molly and Cameron finished breakfast in the dining room of the Grand Hotel. He stopped the rig in front of Tulley's General Store and went in with the list of things Shorty wanted. Shorty was doing a heap of mumbling about how fast the girl went through the supplies. Ned added salt and pepper to the list.

"Got it, Ned?"

Ned bounced the 42-pound sack of flour to his shoulder, his eyes focused on Tulley's carefully trimmed white handlebars. French Creek's Mayor was nothing if not distinguished-looking. "Got it."

Tully rounded the corner of the counter. The bell tinkled as he opened the door for Ned. He followed Ned out. "Wonder what the commotion's about?"

Ned dropped the sack into the buckboard next to all Molly's baby needs. "Didn't hear you."

Tully shaded his eyes with one hand, and pointed with the other.

On the far side of the street just beyond The Egyptian was a spring wagon. A crowd was gathering round.

Tully hurried inside. He grabbed his hat, flipped the open sign and slammed the door. He dashed across the street. Ned followed.

"Someone git Miss Alma," a voice in the crowd shouted. A man Ned knew to be a bachelor went running; most of the women present had their eyes peeled on their husbands.

Ned looked over everyone's heads, but couldn't see much. He pushed through the townsfolk. It was Kate. He hadn't seen her since she left Miss Alma's place. She looked better then. Now her face was distorted; her swollen tongue was thrust over blue lips, and her neck was rope burned. Ned reached a hand around the gawking boy in front of him and pulled the blanket up over her face.

"The show's over, folks," Sheriff said as he nudged through the crowd, belly-first. "Mayor Tulley." He nodded.

Tulley nodded back. "Sheriff."

They stood toe-to-toe. Pristine Tulley standing ramrod straight was a good foot taller than the short rotund sheriff. The fleshy-faced sheriff, inept at best as sheriff, seemed nothing short of slovenly compared to the English-squire appearance of the mayor. A corner of the sheriff's shirttail was out and hanging below his leather vest, the vest was missing two of the three buttons and there was a multitude of pinholes around the crooked star. His formless black felt hat could stand a good brushing. His red moustache was in need of a trim and his pistol was grimy.

The sheriff moved on to the driver. The driver used to be a cowhand for the Rocking J before marriage turned him into a homesteader. "What happened, Tucker?"

Tucker spat tobacco juice over the front of the spring wagon, the only place not crowded with merchants and onlookers. "Found her hanging from a cottonwood at her place down on Dry Gulch Creek."

Ned was wondering what he was doing at Kate's place with a wife at his own.

"More than likely strung up by her cattle-rustlin' friends," Sheriff offered. Then loudly, to the crowd. "Men, I'm gettin' up a posse. Deputize some of you boys to go down and bring in that Tate scoundrel down in the Hole-in-the-Wall."

Ned felt Miss Alma beside him. He got between her and the body. "You don't need to look."

She strained against him to see over his shoulder. "Who's under the blanket?"

"Kate." Ned heard a gasp catch in her throat. "She's been hanged. They're goin' after someone named Tate."

Miss Alma whirled around and sprang like a mountain lion on the unsuspecting sheriff. "You plumb loco, Judd? Tate may be a low-down varmint, but he wouldn't have done that to Kate. Kate was his meal ticket."

The sheriff scratched his red-splotched neck. "I ah, I ah...."

She turned back to Ned. "Kate left me because she was so in love with the man that she would have done anything for him."

"If'n he didn't do it, who—?" The sheriff left the thought hanging.

To Ned's way of thinking there wasn't a soul present who couldn't figure it out, besides the sheriff. Not that anyone was about to cast suspicion out loud. Kate was taking in stolen cattle, everyone knew. Now that Jennings was dead no one could keep Page from doing what he'd been swearing to do, hang every rustler in the territory. Page was making his move.

"See that she gets the best," Miss Alma said to the undertaker. She didn't wait for a reply; instead she turned and walked away.

Ned saw a glow in the undertaker's eyes. He understood what she was saying; she was going to pay. Unless Ned missed his mark, Kate was going to have the fanciest funeral this town had seen for quite some time. Ned suspected the undertaker would even hire professional mourners; his sisters could put any acting troupe to shame.

"Show's over. Go on about your business."

Ned moved off in the wave of dispersing personages. Molly

was standing by the buckboard, staring after Miss Alma. Cameron was lounging in the awning shade fronting the Grand Hotel, nursing what Ned imagined to be a glorious hangover. Ned went into the store behind Tulley. The Rocking J's supplies were still piled high on the counter. Ned had noticed the stock boy in the crowd, explaining why the supplies weren't in the buckboard. Ned scooped up the largest of the four box crates. Business was picking up and he wanted to get Cameron and Molly out of town.

Two women blocked his path. He nodded and skirted round them. They giggled behind black kid gloves.

Tulley ran to the door, but Molly opened it first and stepped in. "Ned, come outside a minute."

He propped the door open with his foot to let her out ahead of him.

"See that woman?" She pointed out Miss Alma.

"The one crossing the footbridge?"

"Yes. Do you know who she is?"

"She's awfully far away." He dropped his load into the back of the buckboard. "Why?" he asked despite himself.

"From the back she looks like my Aunt Carrie."

"Don't rightly know all the townsfolk." He brushed past and reentered the store. The women giggled again.

"You really paid two hundred dollars for a box dinner?" Tulley asked as the women turned away, pretending interest in a bolt of red gingham.

"Many hands make light work." Ned picked up two of the boxes. Tulley winked at the women, and then lifted the last box and followed him out.

The distance had almost swallowed Miss Alma up, but Molly was still looking after her. "Isn't that the strangest thing?"

Ned and Tully put the last of the order in the back. "Thanks for the help," he said to Tulley.

"Think I understand now." Tulley winked. "A bargain at twice the price."

Molly gave Ned a quizzical look after Tulley returned to the store. "What was that all about, suh?"

Ned put his hand at the small of her back. "Come on in, I'll buy you a peppermint."

Molly gave him a knowing grin. "*Pepper*mint?"

Chapter Fifteen
Molly

Molly had worn a path through the green and pink paisley rug in the parlor from her frequent trips to the window. She pulled back the lace curtain; the pouring rain wasn't letting up.

Five long days had passed since her last trip to the Benton homestead. She found solace in knowing that O'Malley was there. She liked the boy and Ned had attested to his character. Still, she worried.

She managed to play two Bach arias at the Spinet before peeking out of the lace curtains again. Straining, Molly made out a yellow-slickered rider bent against the storm. When he was closer, she recognized the rider as Ned. Across the pommel of his saddle was a scrawny calf.

Molly threw a tarp over her head and raced to the end of the porch. The horse disappeared behind flapping doors of the barn. She dashed into the fierce, bitter cold spring storm to follow it.

Ned slid with lanky ease down his horse, the damp and curly calf in hand. She came in and secured the blowing doors. He placed the calf on a pile of hay in one of the stalls. "His ma's dead," Ned said, rising. "Drowned."

Molly dropped to her knees beside the calf and covered him with the hay. She didn't look up at the dripping man. "Will he live?"

"His chances are improving now that you're taking him under wing. Don't usually bring the little things back. Don't have time to worry about every little dogie."

"Why this one?"

"Maybe we can try feeding him through an old glove until he's willing to drink from the bucket. I'll look around the bunkhouse for an odd one."

"How long?" She ran her hand over his white face. He was all black except for white in two spots, the other embarrassed her some.

A bolt of lightning jagged down the western sky, thunder rumbling. Ned steadied his sidestepping, snorting horse. A firm grasp and soft words consoled him until the thunder boxcarred. The sorrel's nostrils flared as he bucked. "Behave yourself," Ned snarled, pulling sharply on the bridle.

"It's not fit for man nor beast." Molly pressed her body against the shaking calf. "What happend to the ones you don't have time for? Will another cow take them in?"

"Not usually."

"What happens to them?"

Ned paused too long. She looked up, demanding an answer.

"We club them over the head."

She tightened her grip, feeling the pounding of its little heart. She envisioned Ned smashing it over the head until it's skull was bashed in.

"They suck with their heads up. Hard to get them to put their heads down in the bucket."

She wasn't listening to him, her blood boiled with anger. "Reason enough to..." She held the rest of her sarcastic tongue.

He sighed. "Need to search for a glove."

Soon the barn was a mix of noises from the rain-soaked wranglers returning from Deadwood with more horses for the company's remuda. Ned had explained that, with the hands starting work at four and finishing after dark, they were each using up four or five horses a day. A man could work harder than a beast.

Along with the roar of thunder and flash of lightning the barn filled with sounds of horses whinnying at the removal of water-heavy saddles, and men happy to be sheltered from the black storm.

Molly, at one of the boy's suggestions, coaxed the calf to suck on a piece of rag coated with milk. Feeding the calf turned into a tedious job, repeated around the clock every two hours. Her anger at the practice of clubbing of orphaned calves lessened with each feeding.

Two days later when the sun was in a bright blue sky and the mud was drying up, Molly was torn between the calf and the Bentons. She hadn't seen Ned, who left the bunkhouse before dawn and got back after dark each day, since lashing out at him about the clubbing. He sent a cowboy to the house with a glove once one was finally found. The calf was her responsibility, the way she saw it, and until he said otherwise, she'd care for it.

She was unsuccessful in getting Cameron to feed the calf, but was able to sweet-talk Shorty into helping. He was gruff only to the bottom layer of skin, under that, he was pure gold.

O'Malley had returned to the Rocking J the previous day. He assured her that the Bentons were fine. The well was up and working, the Rocking J milk cow was secured behind the new fence, and Mrs. Benton seemed to be getting her strength back. Timmy was able to do the chores alone now.

Molly filled a sack with fresh bread, chicken and a batch of sugar cookies. She tied it to her saddle. When she untied it at the Benton's, Timmy came running.

"Ma's sick." His eyes danced with fear.

She handed him the reins and ran into the cabin. Molly dropped the sack and rushed to the bed. She pulled aside the flour-sack curtain and cast her eyes on the feverish woman. Blood trickled from the corner of her mouth to a stained circle on the pillow. Molly placed her hand on Annie's forehead. The searing heat passed through Molly's glove. The woman coughed in spasms, staining her lips.

"Here." Timmy handed Molly a water compress made from diaper cloth. Molly put it on the hot forehead. Out of her mind with fever, Annie threw it off. Molly wiped her face and throat with it.

"Leave it alone, Annie." She had to go for the doctor. "Timmy, honey, sit here with her. Keep doing this to keep the fever down."

She left them, only to become aware of the two crying, hungry babies. Who was to feed the babies? Molly threw up her hands.

"Timmy, do you think you could ride my horse all the way to town and fetch the doctor?"

His bottom lip trembled bravely. "I could, but the doctor won't come. He's for cattle barons and the townsfolk. He won't see nesters."

"Homesteaders," she corrected. "All right. I'll go for him."

Molly sent him for fresh milk while she raced between Annie and the babies. She added a pinch of sugar to the milk and then soaked a clean diaper cloth in it. She touched the cloth to Ruth's cheek. Ruth immediately turned her greedy mouth to it. Her eyes grew big. "Even a newborn baby knows a trick when its presented," she told Timmy as they laughed at the funny face Ruth made.

"It's not Ma's milk, is it, Ruthy?"

Hunger prevailed and, with some misgivings, she sucked the milk from the cloth. "Hyeh, you take hold of it now." Timmy took her place in the rocking chair. She handed him the baby. "Just keep dipping it into the milk."

Having assured herself that Timmy could handle the babies, Molly started her long journey to town. The afternoon sun worked its way west and by and by got under the brim of her hat and burned her pale cheeks. Molly kept drumming the horse's ribs. Time was of the essence.

Though the sky was still light, the sun had slipped behind the rugged Big Horns by the time she jumped from the saddle in front of the doctor's office. The housekeeper answered the bell only to inform Molly that Doc was at the saloon. She hurried to the saloon. There she was told that they hadn't seem him and to try Miss Alma's. She coaxed the directions out of the bear-like bartender.

Molly rode her played-out horse to the two-story, white framed house. There was only a narrow strip of crimson-red light over the mountains but Molly could see the house well enough. It had the inviting look of a Southern home. The two-sided, vine-covered veranda was supported by white columns, and the lush green grass, bushes, and blossoming lilacs added color. The house was shaded by big willows.

The door was opened by an elderly Negro. The anxiety written on his face must have mirrored her own. Molly asked for the doctor between gasps for air. The Negro turned as if looking for the doctor. Molly pushed passed him and rushed in. It was only when she reached the bar that she stopped and looked around. Suddenly it dawned on Molly that Miss Alma's was not a boarding house. Keeping her eyes riveted on the floor, instead of on the scantily clad woman sitting on the lap of a cowboy, she called out for the doctor.

"Over here." He was waving a hand in the air and fingering his black string tie with the other.

All eyes were on her as she threaded her way through the tables. "You need to come with me to the Benton's." She held her hand on her chest as though it helped her breathe. "Mrs. Benton is delirious with fever."

He rose and pulled out a chair for her. "Now hold on a minute. Sit down and catch your breath."

Molly obliged.

A deep furrow appeared between his massive brows under his wire-rimmed spectacles. "Benton? Benton? Seems I've heard that name, but can't rightly place them."

"They live close to the Rocking J," Molly was able to say between breaths.

A woman appeared with a glass of water. "Hyeh, honey, drink this."

Molly looked up at the woman as she took the water. "Thank you." She gulped the water. It was the woman from the street, the one Ned didn't know. Not only was the resemblance to Aunt Carrie striking, but the voice was so much like her mother's. And tall! It was just a flutter of a thought, unformed in words, but instinctively Molly knew who she was. She turned her eyes down to keep the knowledge hidden.

The doctor took off his specs and pulled out a handkerchief. He fogged the lenses with his breath and wiped them clean. "Nesters?" The hardness in his voice told her that Timmy had been right about him.

"Homesteaders," said Molly defensively, watching him tug the ear-piece to settle it behind his red ear. "If you're worried about your fee, I'll oblige you."

"It's not that," he said, holding up his hands as if to stop her words. "If I treat nesters, the cattlemen—"

"Cattlemen? You mean Page, don't you?"

"Doc," the woman's drawl was softer than before, as if equalizing Molly's harsh words, "why don't you ride along out with her?" It was more of a command than a question.

"Sure thing, Miss Alma." The Doc tossed down his drink, plopped his hat on his thinning blond hair, and rose.

Although she couldn't meet the woman's eyes, Molly looked up into her face and thanked her.

By the time the buggy was hitched and her horse tied on, Molly was certain of it. The woman was her Aunt Missy. Aunt Missy's real name started with an A. She was sure of it. While waiting for Mark, Luke, and John to join Matthew, her grandparents had filled the house with girls. A-something,

Beatrice, Carrie, and Deedra. She remembered her aunts and mother laughing about how their mother refused to add an E to the household in search of Mark.

Why had she written all those lies? The chandelier over the diningroom table, she supposedly bought in Venice during her honeymoon in Europe. The hand-painted china. The piano. All lies.

At least she cared enough to keep in touch with her family. Maybe in the letters home, she was able to find some kind of solace from her hideous life. In a way, Molly could understand why she pretended to be something she wasn't. How would she have been able to tell her sisters what she really was? It was the kindest thing she could have done. If she hadn't written, her sisters would have spent their whole lives worrying. As for their visit to the West, they hadn't been invited. It wasn't as if she purposefully set out to deceive them. Molly could understand and forgive her aunt's deception. But what of Ned's part?

She listened to the turning of the wheels along the dark dirt path. The howling of coyotes and other eery night sounds made her spine tingle. The landscape illuminated by the moon had grown desolate. A hopelessness had crept into the night, weighing down her heart.

There was a glow of light spilling through the cracks in the door when they arrived. Inside she found Ned lifting his sleepy head from the table. He pushed the chair back and rose to meet her.

"What are you doing here?" she whispered.

"When you didn't return home for supper, Cameron and I came looking for you."

The cradles were missing. Timmy's bed was empty. She pushed the flour-sack curtain back. The feather tick was pulled up over Annie's face. "She's dead." Molly was just barely aware of Ned standing behind her, his arms turning her around.

"We've taken the children to the Rocking J. There wasn't anything anyone could do for her." She buried her head in his chest. The strain of the day fell back on her and she sobbed.

Ned patted her back. "Doc, we'd be obliged if you'd come to the Rocking J and look at the babies for us."

Chapter Sixteen
Page

The week-long rain had slowed progress. But Page was determined to rid the valley of the no-account squatters. Starting with persuading the ones nearest the Circle 8, along the south end of the open range, to find a better place to live. Then when he married Miss Molly, he'd move out the squatters along French Creek, the northern border. The ring was here now. Tomorrow he would make the trip to the Rocking J.

More important than the ring's arrival was that of the new men. They wouldn't be drawing hands' wages, but shootists'. They would rid the valley of the rustling varmints. Make the valley a decent place again.

"Riders comin'," Saint said, poking his head around the corner of the library door.

Page followed him to the porch.

Five riders, horse hooves drumming in unison, made their way to his big red house. They reined in tight, horses stopping in their tracks.

The shaggy-haired cutthroat, flanked by the other four, spoke out of the side of his mouth. A jagged scar gave his mouth a perpetual snarl. "Lookin' for Franklin Page."

"You've found him." Page eyed the men hard. They had to be the hired guns. The wires said that the special boxcar from Cheyenne was side-railed in Casper and the Texas men were unloading.

"Tom Nash." The scarfaced man leaned over his saddle to look down the row. "That there's just plain Injun, this here's Stretch," turning in his saddle, Tom pointed at the stubble-whiskered man on his other side, "Hank, and that there's Lefty."

Lefty spat a stream of brown juice.

Page eyed the group with uncertainty. "I count five." They looked rough, but they weren't enough. "Paid for twenty-two."

Tom gave a half-smile. "Fact is, you ain't paid for nothin', yet." He slouched easy in his saddle. "Rest are with the wagon. Should be here tomorrow, or day after."

Page turned to Saint. "See that they're settled in, then bring them to me."

He was looking over the ledger in the library when the trail-worn men appeared an hour later following Saint.

"Have a seat," Page called out from behind the big oak desk that had been shipped all the way from Saint Louis. He scowled as the five new men sat on his expensive furniture with the same care as mongrels. Page pushed himself away from the desk, got up and walked around to the front.

"As I told you, Tom, in my letter, we've been plagued by rustlers." He struck a match and looked over the yellow flame to the rugged men. Page touched the match to his imported Havana cigar, drawing deeply. The Injun was slouched so low on the couch that Page feared his black hair would leave a grease spot. He cleared his throat when Lefty started to raise his spurred boot to the ottoman. The man wasn't bright enough to perceive it as a warning. "Saint here has the list. You and your men are to persuade those rustlers to return my cattle."

Tom's icy green eyes told Page he understood.

"While you're at it, boys," Page said, "persuade the

squatters to find a better place to live. Can't grow crops here, but they're just not smart enough to know what's good for them.''

Tom stared right through him. Page knew him by reputation. The man would do whatever he was hired to do. No compunctions. Page wanted the valley cleared out, this man would clear it out. He would have no qualms about resettling folks. Boothill was full of folks he had resettled.

Page was about to ask if they'd settled in well. But before he had the chance, Tom had the audacity to put his hat on and signal to the men. He rose and straightened the holster at his hip, fingering the Colt .44. "We'll start right away."

Chapter Seventeen
Peaches

Lightning struck on the McPhearson homestead the year before, burning the cabin to a charred shell. A new one was built by friends and neighbors just over the hill. Peaches, the sixteen-year-old daughter, had trouble understanding a lot of things, including the fact that the family had moved.

She had been out picking wild flowers, became turned around and found herself back at the burnt-out place. Before she got much of a chance to cipher what to do, she heard shooting.

Peaches ran into the burnt shell and crouched low to look out through a gaping hole between two cindered logs. She saw riders. Too many to count on one hand. They were killing her father's cows. Just as bold as day.

One cow caught her eye. The cow was hit, but still managed to scramble off. Two riders gave chase. They trapped the cow pretty close to the old house. Peaches heard one of the men say, "Don't kill her just yet." He raised his six-shooter and shot off a tit, then another. The cow ran, leaving the man with a moving target. The next shot hit the bag. The cow's cry was so sad.

Peaches narrowed her eyes at the two men slouching in their saddles. They were laughing at the poor cow's misery.

She put down her bouquet and picked up a stone. She ran

out of the burnt cabin. She got behind the man that done all the shooting, and threw the stone hard. The stone thudded against his neck. The man howled. Now he knew what misery felt like. It wasn't a laughing matter. And he wasn't laughing.

He jerked around in his saddle and shot, just missing her. Peaches threw herself on the ground. But he didn't shoot again. Instead he put his gun in his holster.

"Well, now, what'a we got ourselves, here?"

There was something about him that scared her. She got up and ran away from him.

"Git her, Stretch," yelled the man she hit in the neck.

The two horses surrounded her in no time at all. They pranced, side-stepped, whinnied, jerked their heads and pushed their tongues against the bits. They snorted and blew snot out their noses. The men laughed like they did at the cow.

Peaches tried to skirt around the horse in front of her, but each time, the horse would jump in front of her. She could feel the man behind her slide from his horse. His hands yanked her around. All the time she heard shots in the distance.

"My, aren't you a feisty one."

"Go on, Lefty, teach her some manners."

Her mother had already taught her manners. She also knew how to set the dinner table.

Lefty threw off his cartridge belt, his eyes gawking at her like she was stark naked.

"Go away!"

He shook his head slowly. He leaned over her until the wind-bent clump grass was brushing her back and then jerked her legs out from under her. Her head thumped against the ground.

She screamed and swiped her fingernails across his cheek as he smeared her face with his wet lips.

He grabbed her wrist and twisted it so fast she heard the bone snap before she felt the pain. All the time he kept wetting her face with his tongue. She screamed until she was out of breath. The pain shot all the way up her arm.

The other man laughed as the one who had been licking her threw her skirt and petticoat over her head. The one doing all the laughing held her hands over her head, and dug his dirty nails into her flesh. Her broken wrist throbbed and shot pain every time she tried to move. Her underclothes were ripped away as she kicked and squirmed to free herself.

Peaches stopped screaming to spit the cottony-tasting skirt material out of her mouth. Each time she sucked air the skirt clung to her nose and mouth. She tried hard to listen to the two men. They were laughing and saying things about her that she knew her father wouldn't like. She would have to listen better to their words so she could repeat them like her father always told her to.

The one knocked the breath out of her as he fell down on top of her.

"Your face is too pretty to hide." He yanked her skirts down from over her head and tucked them under his belly.

It was a little easier to breath until he started kissing her. Then she was sucking the foul air from the cavity of his mouth. She bit his lip hard enough to taste blood.

"You little bitch." He raised up and wiped his hand across his mouth and looked at the smear of blood. He struck her across the face, hurting her.

And frightening her.

"Stick it to her," the other cheered.

He frightened her, too.

His knee bore down just below her chestbone, pushing her even farther into the dirt and expelling what little air was in her lungs. They stung from not getting air. She needed to breathe. He moved his knee. She gasped for air as his rough hands tore her dress to the waist in a zigzag manner. It was a bad tear and would be hard to mend. He twisted one of her nipples and bit the other. She screamed and screamed, and screamed again when her wrist shot pain up to her elbow.

She managed to turn her leg just so and kicked him in the back. He pinned her legs down and then started pinching the tender flesh between her thighs.

She strained and twisted, but couldn't free herself.

He poked his fingers inside her as he fumbled with his breeches.

She shut her eyes tight and clenched her teeth as he stretched his full weight over her. A long, sharp, ripping pain came between her legs as he pushed something into her. Her inners cramped with a pressure she couldn't recognize. Everything was happening so fast. He snorted like a pig as he pushed back and forth, back and forth, over and over again. She screamed as he caused a quick sharp stinging pain deep inside her. Sweat rolled off his face and dripped on her. It was so hard to catch her breath. She cried and begged him to stop.

Then he cried out, and stopped.

She thought he might be dead.

He wasn't.

Peaches took a deep breath as he rolled off. She turned her head to the side, feeling the scratchy grass on her cheek and nose.

The men changed places. This one needed a bath even more. She felt her lungs collapse against the weight. Again she felt the stinging pressure of the pushing in and out, in and out, in and out. Then, like the first, the second suddenly stopped with a groan. He didn't roll off, he just collapsed on top of her.

Peaches found her troubles weren't over. There was a circle of riders now, each wanting a turn at her. She listened to their ugly remarks as she pushed her head farther into the clump-grass to hide her shame. The pain turned dull and annoying, like chafing from coarse drawers. She wondered if the cow would die from its wounds or if her father would butcher it. She cried thinking about the cow long after the horses galloped away.

Chapter Eighteen
Molly

The doctor had sent away to Denver for nursing-bottles, but in the meantime Molly had fashioned two out of her soft kid gloves, pricking a hole in the middle, and longest, finger. Reluctantly, the hungry babies gave in to the foreign taste of both the leather and the milk.

Timmy had been a big help to Molly. He'd taken over the responsibility of feeding the calf during the day. Molly wouldn't hear of him doing it at night. A growing boy needed his sleep.

She had carried the lantern out to the barn last night at two to find Ned talking to the calf. He had dipped his finger in the bucket of milk and had gotton the calf to suck on it, but when he tried to coax it into putting its head in the bucket, the calf rebelled.

Molly laughed as she thought of how crimson he turned when he realized she had caught him talking to a critter. "Molly you git back to the house," Ned had said over his shoulder, trying to hide his blush. "The babies are enough for you. The boys'll see to the calf."

Ned had been putting in such long days that she felt guilty. He was such a kind hearted person. And a liar. Molly cuddled Naomi closer to her as the baby sucked the glove.

What would become of the babies? Or Timmy? Her aunt

didn't own the Rocking J; they were there only through the goodness of the foreman. The foreman who lied to her, saying he didn't know who the woman, Alma, was. There was no hope for a future on the Rocking J. Nor hope of Aunt Missy giving Cameron money for the business.

Molly heard the commotion down in the yard. It was a visitor, employees wouldn't ride into the yard. Perhaps it was the doctor with the nursing bottles. Her interest was keen, but she didn't dare rise to look out the bedroom window. She listened to the low voices at the door, and then the quick footsteps on the stairs. Timmy's.

"Mr. Page is here to see ya."

Heavy bricks weighted her shoulders. Page's visit was somewhat akin to Euripides' *deus ex machina*, though not all of them would be delivered into the hands of the gods. One of them would find ungodly chubby, tobacco-stained hands, she feared. "Thank you, Timmy. Tell him to have a chair in the parlor. I'll be down as soon as I am able."

"Mr. Stewart's seeing to him," the boy added gaily.

Do tell. "Thank you, Timmy. Tell my brother I'll be down as soon as I finish with this baby.

When Naomi drifted off to sleep, Molly placed her in the cradle. She checked her appearance in the glass mirror, touching the tips of her fingers to her tongue then running her hands over her hair to calm the wild fringes. It would have to do.

Her brother was raising a whiskey glass to Page just as she entered the room. "Molly dear." He tossed down the drink. "Well, I'll leave the two of you alone." Cameron's glance penetrated through her like acid. There was no mistaking what he wanted.

When he was gone, Molly greeted the big man sitting on the green velvet settee with a smile. Not only out of politeness, but in amusement at seeing how he had groomed himself for the visit. "How nice to see you, suh."

He set his whiskey glass down on the mahogany three-legged table at his arm, hard enough that the kerosene in the lamp sloshed. Page patted the velvet next to him. "Come here, Molly gal."

Steeling herself, Molly crossed the room and sat on the edge of the crowded settee.

Page took a jeweler's box from his inside breast pocket and handed it to her.

She opened the box with shaky hands. Inside was a large sparkling solitaire diamond. Molly swallowed hard. She was determined to keep depression from gaining full control.

"Why Mr. Page, this is the most beautiful diamond I have ever seen." She smiled at him. The arrogance in his eyes caused her to turn away.

"It's the biggest they had."

Molly framed a smile on her face. "It's lovely." She gently closed the lid as she rose. She paced and thought.

At last she sat on the edge of the settee. "Mr. Page, I don't love you." She sensed him stiffening. "But if you're willing to still have me and willing to make a home for Timmy and his two baby sisters, I will marry you."

"Timmy, the sandy-haired boy that fetched you down?"

Molly nodded.

"Have no objection to him, can always use an extra hand."

"Not a hand, he'll need proper schooling."

He cleared his throat and nodded heartily. "No, no. You misunderstood. Not a hand. School. Yes, school."

"And his twin sisters."

"School, of course. The best schooling money can buy."

"When they are old enough, you mean?"

"Yes, when they are old enough." He folded her fingers over the ring box. "Bring them."

He seemed so ready to agree. Perhaps everything would work out for the best. The children would have a permanent place to live. Cameron and their mother would have Father's company back. Ned would be rid of the uninvited guests and Aunt Missy wouldn't be found out.

"When would...were you planning the ceremony?"

"Tomorrow's as good a day as any," he said, rising and putting on his Stetson.

Panic bolted through her. She took a cleansing breath. What difference did it make really? Tomorrow wasn't any worse than the day after, or the week after, or the month after, or the year after. Sooner or later the day would come. "Tomorrow then," she said bravely.

He stopped at the door. "I'll send someone after your things early in the morning."

Molly nodded. She was relived to see him leave without kissing her. Though she didn't expect him to be as generous tomorrow.

Chapter Nineteen
Saint

Saint wasn't all-fired up over the new men. They weren't needed. He could shoot as well as any of them, he was as certain of that as night follows day. If Page had wanted more guns, he should have sent him down to Cheyenne to hire some. Or Denver. He could have gathered up as good a group of gunman as the Texas gang. He would have seen to it that his men understood they could do a little ranch work to boot. Something the Texans found beneath them.

He and Blacky spent days with cinch rings, rebranding the cattle returned from Kate's place. The Rocking J's brand had always been simple to change to Circle 8; Double D was harder. Those not branded, all of them milky-breathed, were the easiest, of course. Those few with squatters' brands that he couldn't figure a way to change, were rotting carcasses now.

It would have taken a sight less time if Blacky hadn't been babying his sore hand. And one heck shorter time if the Texans had offered a hand.

As far as Saint knew, the only thing the new men had done was find bunks. That they made simple work of. They found five bottom bunks in a row and threw their plunder on them. The fact that the bunks were already claimed didn't seem to faze them much. It was just a matter of heaping the old belongings together in the center aisle.

Still, his work wasn't done. Now Page wanted him to follow the shootists to town to make certain they stayed out of trouble. Page said he couldn't afford to have the townsfolk up in arms and siding with squatters.

Saint and Blacky found the men at the saloon. Injun was teaching a odd-looking stranger how to dance to his gun. The stranger was dressed in a long black coat buttoned all the way to his chin. His black hat was flat. Saint and Blacky ordered two-bit whiskey—they liked to ease their way into the cheaper rot-gut whiskey—and ambled over to Tom's table.

"Who's the stranger with Injun?" Saint asked.

Left answered. "Some Quaker fella trying to peddle cure-all."

"That so?" Blacky cupped his right hand and gave the tiniest of moans.

Saint wasn't certain what to make out of it. Sam was playing jumping music and Harry was tending bar like nothing was out of the ordinary. He looked over to Tom. "What's the story?"

Tom took a swig from a bottle of whiskey and leaned his chair back on two legs. Saint took it to mean the story was forthcoming in epic detail. "When we got to town the Quaker man was addressing the crowd round his carnival wagon. Sellin' Chickasaw Indian remedies." He pointed a finger at Injun. "Injun was all taken in. Just know'd it was the real thing, being as though it said so right there on the label and all—"

"Injun cain't read," Lefty interrupted.

Tom righted his chair and stared hard at Lefty. "You tellin' the story or me?"

Lefty stopped laughing at his little joke and scratched at the scales in his beard. "You are, Tom."

The good side of Tom's lip curled into a smile. "Couldn't tell fer the way your mouth was running." He tipped his chair back. "Anyways." He nodded at the dancing man. "He said it cured all ails. Didn't think he would lie, being a Quaker man and calling folks 'friends', 'brothers and sisters'—''

"Every sentence was full of 'thee' and 'thou'," Lefty offered.

Tom righted his chair with a bang.

Lefty covered his mouth.

Tom leaned back. "Injun's gun arm's been stiff of a mornings, last couple years."

"Reckon it's on account of the three bullet holes." Stretch hooked a finger through the handle of his half-empty beer mug and hastened to the bar before Tom had a chance to reprimand him.

"Anyhow, Injun bought the medicine. Said the thickness didn't suit him, took a long time goin' down the gullet, coating it all the way. He gave it about as much time to work as it takes a rattler to strike."

"He's not noted for his patience." Lefty grabbed his mug and was off. Hank followed, through he hadn't opened his mouth to do anything but spit toward the cuspidor. Saint hoped his aim with a six-shooter was better.

"The Quaker man was too busy selling to give Injun the time of day 'cept to say, 'Thee's a big man. Try another dose.' Injun did just that, and another, and another. The bottle was empty and still he felt his arm pain, and didn't like the taste in his mouth. He told the feller so."

The Quaker screamed and grabbed his boot and hopped around one-legged. Injun nicked a toe, Saint surmised.

" 'Thee needs to give it some time to work, Brother' the Quaker man said. This bothered Injun powerful. Probably remembering how the Quaker fellow said it took effect immediately. He said that before he bought it. After, it didn't. He got to figgerin' and wondered what else it didn't do." Tom took another swig. "Anyhow, that's how the Quaker man came to be learning to dance."

Saint tired quickly of the infernal shooting, and was just

about to say so when Sam started playing something that took Tom's fancy. Tom started tapping his foot, and then, hooking his thumbs under his gun belt, called to Injun. "Reckon, he's plumb tired, Injun. Best be buying the man a friendly drink, now."

Injun stopped shooting and leered at the shaking Quaker, then turned to the bartender. "Git the man a drink."

Harry wiped his hands on his chest and asked the Quaker what he wanted with about as much enthusiasm as a man going to his own hanging.

The Quaker man jawed some, but nothing came out of his mouth.

"What's that?" the bartender asked. "Couldn't hear ya."

"Thou...thou hav'st a bottle of beer?" for a golden-tongued medicine man, he seemed a bit tongue-tied, and not necessarily from dancing.

The bartender took out a quart bottle of beer. "Plumb amazing." He blew off the dust, "second time this month someone's asked for one." He set it on the bar. "Eight bits."

Injun's eyes got big as saucers. "Ain't payin' no eight bits fer no beer." He leveled his gun and shot the Quaker through the heart. "Reckon he don't need it no how."

The barter shook his head. "Should've asked for a draw," he said, as he put his lips to the quart bottle.

Saint tossed down his drink. "Reckon it's time we was headin' towards Miss Alma's whorehouse."

An overwhelming majority of the men favored the idea. In unison, drinks were tossed down.

Tom stopped at the bar on the way out. He laid his hand on Injun's forearm just as the Indian brought his mug to his lips. "Injun, you've had enough. Make yerself skreece."

"You tellin' me I can't hold my liquor?"

Tom snarled at him. "The Chickasaw remedy was two hundred proof, I 'spect. You had a whole bottle of it before you bellied up to the bar.''

"Didn't taste like no liquor to me." Injun spat into the pool of blood widening around the Quaker man.

Chapter Twenty
Doc

The Blue Lodge at the Masonic Temple on the far side of French Creek was adjourning to The Egyptian for refreshments. Having a gurgling creek running through town made a lot of things easier, fishing to name one. The meandering stream brought the biggest Rainbows and Browns any angler could hope to snare.

That is, when the spring runoff wasn't in progress. Then, the roar of the rapidly moving water could be heard throughout the town. The winter-hooded Big Horns were shedding their white coats faster than the streams could flow. Coupled with the week-long rains, French Creek swelled above the bridge.

"I'd like to meet up with the man who'd built this here bridge," Gentry, the bank owner, said holding on to the slippery railing as he waded through the ankle-deep murky water.

"Well, turn around then, you fool, and have a look," Mayor Tulley yelled above the roaring water.

Doc suspected Gentry was throwing Tulley that characteristic ugly look of his. Whenever Gentry was disgusted, he'd swallow his chin. Doc's theory was that the man's jaw was double-jointed. It was too dark to see, which Doc knew suited the other men just fine. Most people thought looking at Gentry's face in its normal state could ruin their day.

"Ah *Mayor* Tulley," Yates called. Some of his Masonic brothers thought Tulley had gotten high and mighty over his title. "It were your pa done built it," the postman reminded as he winked to the undertaker. "Might have raised it some, if'n you ask me."

"Which no one did," snapped the mayor.

The sheriff cupped his hands around his mouth. "You boys comin' cross or what? Always bickering over something or other," he added in a lower voice.

"Hold your hosses, Sheriff. It's a mite slippery," Gentry hollered back. "Water's soaked clear through my boots."

"Don't have a brain between them," the sheriff said to Doc and Duncan, the livery man.

The doc breasted his specs. They were wet from all the splashing, besides not wanting them falling off his nose in case he slipped. He wished Judd wouldn't talk about his brothers in that fashion. He'd like to see him take his obligation more seriously. "Square yourself, Brother." The doc tried to bite back the words, but they were already downstream.

"Be a lot easier bein' square with the world if'n the world measured up a sight better."

"Stop being so cranky, Sheriff, Doc was just reminding you of your obligation," Duncan said, spitting chew downstream.

"Don't need no remindin'", the sheriff said, mainly to himself.

When Gentry, Tulley, Yates, and Thaddeus caught up, the fraternal brothers fanned out and counter-marched down the middle of the street. "Awful quiet at the saloon," Yates stated.

Gentry, Tulley, and Yates stood like statues in the doorway. The sheriff pushed through them as if they were the batwings. He stopped dead in his tracks. "Say, Doc, there's a fella in here in need of your services."

Doc threaded around his brothers. He crouched down beside the man. There was no sign of life. Doc unbuttoned the black coat, and the blood-drenched white shirt under it. The puckered bullet hole was aligned with the heart. It was about as clean a wound as he had ever seen, except for a protuding bone shard splintered from the sixth rib. He slid his hand over the man's dull, dilated eyes. "His needs are better serviced by Thaddeus."

Thaddeus, the undertaker, stepped into the blood pool. The tacky blood pulled away in long strings as he picked up his feet. He bent down over the corpse, brushing Doc's shoulder. "No two ways about it." Thaddeus checked the linings of his pockets first thing. He took a nicely clipped bundle of greenbacks.

"Looks like you'll be giving the stranger the very best," Doc said sardonically.

"Surely wouldn't want to shortchange him, bein' he's away from his family and friends and all."

Doc patted Thaddeus on the shoulder as he rose. The thickening blood weighed down his boots as he moved out of the red circle. "You're a good Christian man. I'm sure there's a special place behing the pearly gates just for the likes of you."

Thaddeus furrowed his brows as if he wasn't quite sure how to take that. "A couple you boys help me take him over to my place?"

With great trepidation, Yates and Duncan moved forward, followed by the sheriff.

"Who done this?" the sheriff asked the bartender.

Harry plucked at the garter around his sleeve while he fished for the words. "Stranger, Sheriff. Big mean-lookin' Injun." His face lit up. "Yeah, they called him Injun."

The sheriff leaned against the counter. "They?"

"Real desperados! Maybe six of them."

"You have to get up a posse, Sheriff," the mayor insisted.

"They can't get away with coming into town and killing law-abiding citizens. Even if he was a stranger."

"But if they're desperadoes." The sheriff looked beseechingly at Tulley. The mayor's back was straight. Sheriff sighed. "Which way d'they ride out?"

The bartender scratched his thick eyebrows. "Don't think they did. Seems like Saint took'um on down to Miss Alma's."

Doc watched the sheriff's Adam's apple bob as he swallowed hard. "Saint's with them?"

Duncan inched back. "Reckon I'd best mosey on. Sounds like old Grady'll need another hand with all them new horses."

"Wait a minute," Tulley said. "We came to get a drink. Let's sit down and have that drink. We need to talk this out."

None of the others thought there was much to discuss, knowing these desperados of a minute ago were just new hands of the Circle 8. "Let's do have that drink," Doc echoed.

The bartender lined up the glasses and ran the open bottle over them. Each man took a glass. Tulley carried the bottle.

When they were all settled around the table, Tulley said, "This can't go on. Kate, that Tate feller, McPhearson's daughter, and now this."

Thaddeus nodded. "No-accounts Kate and Tate was one thing, but raping McPhearson's half-wit daughter was uncalled for."

Gentry's pinched-up face eyed Thaddeus hard. "You'd been a sight happier if'n they killed her, like they did Kate. Can hear the silver clinging in your poke even louder if'n they did."

Doc's drink overturned as Thaddeus grabbed Gentry's collar.

"Now, boys," the sheriff said, as he edged between the pair. "Ain't no call to talk like that. Just ease back." He watched their muscles relax. "Now, sit on down." He refilled the glasses. "Now that's right nice."

"Don't rightly see where it's got anyting to do with us. It's between the cattlemen and the squatters." Duncan said after some silent thinking.

Yates tossed down his drink. "McPhearson's daughter's so crazy she might have brought it on herself."

The doc could hear a metallic ring in his voice, but said nothing.

Thaddeus nodded as if he'd like to believe that. "This here fella's a stranger." Thaddeus fingered the new money in his pocket. "Doesn't have anything to do with us."

The conversation died of its own inertia. Soon Tulley and Gentry drifted back to their peaceful homes and waiting families. The sheriff went about his official duties, starting with testing the merchants' locks. Doc followed the blood trail Thaddeus, Duncan, Yates, and the corpse were making as far as his place.

Chapter Twenty-One
Tom

The frogs were tuning up in the lily pond smack dab in the middle of the whorehouse yard. After leaving the horses at the hitching rail, Tom and his men made their way up the path.

"Miss Alma's a close friend of Mr. Page," Saint said so low as to barely be heard above the spurs jingling and boots creaking along the planks of the porch. "He wouldn't want anything bad to happen here."

Tom really wasn't interested in anything the man had to say.

"Miss Alma runs a respectable place. Understand?"

"Don't be gittin' in a flutter. How many times we need to be told?" Tom asked, flexing his hand over the pearl handle of his Peacemaker. "You all behave, ya hear?"

Grumbles came in one voice.

Tom smiled at the man he didn't cotton to, probably because he and his boss were two peas in the same pod. "See, they're all in agreement. Ain't goin' to be no trouble."

Blacky held the door open with his bandaged hand, his face etched in make-believe pain. They filed in.

Lefty grabbed the closest gal, a red-haired beauty with enormous breasts. He half-carried her all the way up the stairs. She didn't look too happy about it. Lefty had no breeding when it came to such matters.

"That was Ginger. This way." Saint pointed toward the bar.

Tom turned to follow him, giving the signal that Stretch and Hank were to come along peacefully.

"Whiskey," Tom hollered to the old colored man as he and his party sat at a round table where they had a view of all the local talent. A gal a piece were at their sides in no time at all.

"Pricilla's my name," a gal told Stretch as she licked his earlobe.

A pretty brunette with a mole—beauty mark—over her lip asked, "You all new hands of Page?"

"Why you think that?" Hank asked.

She pointed to Saint and Blacky. "You with them, ain't you?"

"You could say we work for Page if'n you're a'mind." Tom winked at her. Tom didn't much like spending time talking about the fat cattleman. He knew that after they did Page's bidding, he would holler the loudest to get them out of the territory. They always did. There was no place for a shootist to call home. Nothing at the end of the long trail but a short rope.

She slid down until she was sitting on his lap. "I'm Dixie."

Tom cupped his hand around one of her cheeks—one to the set he wasn't looking at—to keep her from slipping off his lap. "I'm right proud to make your acquaintance. Tom Nash."

Dixie smiled, making the mole halfway disappear under the fold of her turned-up ruby-red lips. He only half-realized the old colored man had brought their drinks. No one else at the table seemed to pay him much attention.

A blond was tickling Hank's ear. "My name's Laura Jean. What's yours?" Laura Jean had the highest, squeakiest voice this side of the Missouri. Hell, both sides.

Hank had to think a minute. Like the rest of them, the shrill made him forget everything else. "Hank. That's bobtail for . . . ah—"

112

"Henry, you fool," Stretch obliged. "Ain't no one don't know that, 'ceptin' maybe a half-wit like yourself."

Hank took exception to that. Flying up, he hit the blond in the eye with his elbow as he pulled back to cold-cock Stretch.

Faces pinched up all around the table. Laura Jean's scream was an octave higher than her voice. A wonder the chandelier was still in one piece.

"That's enough," Tom yelled at the boys. He hoped Laura Jean understood that she was free to quit squawking, too.

The boys backed off. Stretch ruefully rubbed his jaw as Hank led Laura Jean upstairs.

Tom turned his attention back to a more pressing matter. He ran his horn-tough hand over the satin ruffle of Dixie's bodice. "Cain't remember the last time I felt anything so soft."

"You making reference to the satin or to flesh you're squeezing with your hidden hand?" Her eyes crinkled at the corners and her lips rippled in a wide smile.

"I would be remiss if I didn't say both are mighty soft."

"Why don't you have your drink, then I'll show you something real soft upstairs."

He downed his drink in one gulp and hurried upstairs with Dixie on his arm.

Tom didn't pay much attention to the room's decor. And he was far more interested in the warm woman in his arms than the picture of the naked cherub on the lily pond. In the glow of the lamp, the beads of perspiration on the prostitute's white skin sparkled like diamonds. He heard a crack beyond her moans. He hurdled out of bed with the second burst, sending Dixie to the floor. That was instinct. Repeated shots called for an investigation.

The gunfire couldn't have been timed any worse. He struggled to untangle the flailing prostitute and his clothing. Fumbling into his pants and grabbing his gun, Tom hurried downstairs.

In the bar he found Lefty and Stretch leaning way back in their chairs looking up at the gold molding around the ceiling, their hats powdered with plaster. The girls were flanking the old colored man, all of them peeking up from behind the bar. The only one standing in the open was a handsome figure of a woman, with hands resolutely fixed on hips.

"Just what in tarnation y'all think ya'h doing'?" the madam demanded.

Lefty let another shot go. The tailend of the respectable clientele, clothing in hand, pushed through the front door in their effort to meet Blacky and Saint at the hitching post.

"Stop that," she clamored as she clapped her hands.

"There's another," hollered Stretch as he shot toward the riddled molding that threatened to give way. He hit the chandelier, shattering a crystal. The pieces clattered, clanging chaotically as the thing twirled on its chain, the gas pipe undisturbed.

"Look what you've done!"

Stretch turned and shot over the woman's head.

She ducked behind the bar. "What *are* they doing?" the woman asked in a whisper.

Ginger flung a loose red curl over her shoulder. "A nest of wasps are making their way out a crack in the corner. They're gettin' rid of them for ya, Miss Alma."

"That's *just* wonderful." She was looking up at the tinkling light fixture.

Tom called to the men when they stopped to reload. "Stretch, you and Lefty stop this here tomfoolery and head on back to the Circle 8. You've irritated me a heap."

A slope-shouldered Stretch looked like a whipped schoolboy as he holstered his gun and headed for the door. "Didn't mean no harm."

Lefty eyed Tom hard. Tom held his stare. Lefty holstered his gun. He tossed down his drink, then poured another in defiance and gulped it down before sauntering toward the door. His heels clicked across the floorboard. "Cain't even have a little fun no more," Lefty mumbled.

Tom turned and stormed the stairs, two at a time. He didn't like leaving anything unfinished.

Chapter Twenty-Two
Molly

The sun came out bright on Molly's wedding day, casting a long shadow over her. Molly was up before dawn with one of the babies and heard the men ride out. It was for the best, she wasn't up to facing Ned. She would leave a note thanking him for his generous hospitality.

Molly eased herself and the sleeping Ruth out of the rocker, startling the baby but not enough to wake her. Her lucky day. Molly gently placed Ruth in the cradle.

She looked wishfully into the other cradle, wondering how long she would sleep. Sleep had eluded Molly throughout the long night and she suspected that even if both babies slept, she wouldn't. It didn't matter. As she looked on, Naomi's face wrinkled up and her mouth opened, letting rip a screech that could reach the devil himself.

Molly picked up Naomi, cuddled her in the crook of her arm and carried her to the bed to lay her out for the diaper change. Molly wished she had old Mammy to help. Mammy was gone now, hastened by long days and indubitably longer nights of caring for her twin charges, Cameron and Molly.

Many a day Molly had crawled up into Mammy's well-padded lap to hear the stories about the plantation days. She especially liked listening to Mammy tell on her mother. Though Miss Beatrice did little more than follow Aunt Missy around. Aunt Missy seemed to be the culprit in all their pranks.

Molly's favorite story was about Aunt Missy changing dresses with one of the slave children. To hear Mammy tell it, Grandmother jumped clear out of her skin seeing the child in rags. Aunt Missy tried to explain that she had so much and the Negro girl had nothing. The rags were burned, the little girl was allowed to keep Aunt Missy's dress. Aunt Missy's backside was tanned. And Grandmother retired to her bedroom for the rest of the day, complaining of a headache.

Molly carried the fussy baby downstairs. In the kitchen, she found Shorty breaking eggs into a cast-iron frying pan. Cameron was sitting at the table looking on.

"Could I get you to hold Naomi?" Molly asked Cameron as she shoved the baby into his arms. The look of horror on his face brought a smile to hers. "Thank you, suh."

Nitro could not have caused him more discomfort.

"Mighty fine lookin' eggs Timmy found." Shorty tilted the pan and flipped the eggs.

Molly looked over his shoulder. "Mighty fine." She dipped Naomi's glove into the warm milk. "Where is Timmy?"

"Rode out with Ned," Shorty answered, sliding the eggs onto a plate for Cameron.

"Shorty, someone has to ride out and bring him back."

The cook dropped the plate in front of Cameron. "Why's that?"

"We're leaving this morning." She put a pinch of sugar into the milk.

"Leavin'!"

"Molly, will you take this thing off my lap?" Cameron commanded. "My eggs are getting cold."

As if in agreement, Naomi wailed. Molly took the baby from him. "Thank you so very much, Brother dear."

Molly sat down in the chair across from Cameron. Spilt

milk sprayed the baby's cheek. Naomi stopped crying and turned to the glove. She gave it a halfhearted suck and let go. Milk ran free. Molly juggled the baby, pinching off the glove, and sliding out from under the cascading milk.

"Leavin'?" Shorty took the baby.

Molly soaked up the spilled milk with her napkin. "Page is sending a wagon for us—" Her voice cracked. Molly dabbed at her skirt, afraid she'd cry if she said more.

"Visting Circle 8?"

"My sister and Page are marrying," Cameron said between bites.

An egg slipped from Shorty's hand and splattered on the floor.

Cameron wiped his lips on his napkin. "I'll be visiting the Circle 8 for the couple days left of my stay." He tore apart a biscuit and sopped up the runny yolk on his plate. "We won't be back. Though I'm sure Molly will come calling on Aunt Missy when she returns."

"What am I to do with the babies?"

"The three children will be living with us," Molly said softly. She intended to love and rear the children as if they were her own.

Shorty wiped up the egg. "Miss Molly, would ya like some breakfast before I fetch Timmy?"

Molly shook her head. "I'll fix something after I put the baby down." She gave Shorty a smile until she felt her mouth quiver around the edges. "Thank you just the same."

Shorty nodded as he took off his apron. "I'll go for Timmy."

The light was blinding as he opened the door.

Chapter Twenty-Three
Ned

Nothing would be the same again.

Ned swung a leg over the pommel and sat still for a moment studying the swaying cottonwoods fronting the bank of the creek. What a difference water made. Most of the land could grow only clumps of short grass, but at the water's edge the trunks of the trees were lost in a tangle of vine and bush.

He looked over at the boy, riding a saddled horse for the first time in his life. Ned finished rolling his brown-paper cigarette. Timmy was a good boy and deserved better than what he'd got. Ned was determined to see to it that he got better. He struck a match with his thumbnail and touched the sputtering flame to the end of his cigarette. He inhaled deeply, tasting the warm tobacco.

Ned's life had been physically hard. Like Timmy, Ned had been just a youngster when he found himself on his own. He learned the ropes from more experienced hands. At first, he worked on round-ups as a horse wrangler. Then, as he grew and developed muscles and skills, Ned became a full-fledged hand. No one's horsemanship or roping skills were better.

His plunder consisted of no more than what could be carried on his horse. That's how he liked it.

Ned's was a life of a lone man. But now he wanted more.

He wanted Molly. He wanted to do right by Timmy and his sisters. Ned didn't have anything to offer them; no more than what Timmy had when his pa was alive. But for a girl like Molly, he could offer her little besides his love.

Ned had been rolling these thoughts around in his head until his head reeled. He couldn't expect Molly and Cameron to continue living in the big house forever, waiting for Miss Alma's letter to their mother to take hold. Cameron seemed in a mighty hurry to get the money from Page. Besides, he expected the only missive forthcoming would be one by the Kansas City lawyers firing him for letting the pair visit. The pair! Add three children. Everything was busting loose at the seams.

He cast his eyes on the purple mountain range. The Big Horns stood fixed ruggedly above the land, like a sentinel. Men came and went, but the mountains would always be. Hidden there was an extra special parcel of land. It was tucked away in a valley behind the first ridge. There was enough open pasture and water for a good-size herd; enough timber to build a fine house.

Like the rest of the hands, Ned saved little money. His pay was usually blown in one trip to town. But the little he did have, he would spend on cattle. The herd would be small, but in time it would grow. By the time Timmy and his sisters were grown, they'd have something of their own.

Ned was resolved.

There was a hitch. How would he explain the lies and deception to Molly? And then how could he do it without bringing Miss Alma into the picture?

Ned took a deep breath, smelling the camphor of broken sage trampled by hooves. The grazing cattle seemed to swim in the shimmer of the morning sun. Ned told himself that things usually weren't as bad as feared. Things to wrestle with later. Right now he'd see to the here and now.

The boy was watching the cattle drift east, following the

prevailing winds. "You like this life, boy?" Ned asked. "Would you like to have a herd of your own one day?"

"When I grow up, will you let me work here for you?"

Ned heard young bravery in the frail voice. Ned leaned over and jerked down the boy's hat, nothing more than a ragged piece of felt. "You work for me now."

Timmy's eyes were aglow with happiness.

"The boot-up you've got, you'll be the best there is."

"All the men look up to you, Ned. And when I grow up, I want'a be just like you."

Ned leaned back and howled. "Reckon your ma and pa would like you to set your sights a mite higher."

"Don't know why. The way you tried to save pa, the way you took Ruth and Naomi and me in. Pa would be proud to see me do them things."

Ned looked at the boy. To be so pure of heart! "Reckon your Pa's already proud of you." His voice was soft and tender.

Timmy looked away. "I miss Pa powerfully. And Ma even more. It had just been the three of us for so long. There're three again. But it's a mighty powerful burden when the other two in the family are strangers. Even littler than me."

Ned could hear the tears in his voice. "You're doing a find job caring for your sisters."

"Just thankful for Miss Molly and you. Hard telling what would have happened if your buckboard hadn't come along when the well caved in on Pa."

Ned tried not to notice Timmy's heaving shoulders. On the horizon he saw a rapidly approaching rider. Instantly his leg came down from the horn and he whirled around. No one would ride that fast unless it was important. "Timmy, trouble's coming. Be right back," Ned said, throwing the half-finished cigarette into the dirt.

He drummed his horse's ribs. As he drew closer, Ned recognized the rider as Shorty. His heart raced faster than the horse.

Reining in tight, Ned pulled up next to Shorty. "What's wrong?" Ned asked as he watched the old man's chest rise and fall in an attempt to catch his breath. The stable horse blew a steam of mucus from its flaring nostrils.

Shorty coughed. "They're leaving today." He stuck a hand to his gums and coughed again. "I was sent for the boy."

The old man's words came as slow as a calf dragged from a herd at the end of a long rope. "Go on."

"Miss Molly's going to marry Page."

Being gored by a bull wouldn't have hurt as much as Shorty's words. There had to be some mistake, Molly couldn't have agreed to marry him. Not willingly. Cameron was making her do it.

"You see to Timmy," Ned said, reining right. He spurred his horse into the hardest lope the horse had struck in a long time and raced back to the house.

Chapter Twenty-Four
Ned

The lathered horse stopped beside the wagon, its belly heaving, mouth open and nostrils flaring. Looking at the plunder in the two-seated wagon, Ned knew Shorty was telling it straight. He jumped from the horse and ran to the door. He knocked as he pushed the door open.

"Molly!" He tried to keep the frantic urgency he felt from sounding in his voice.

Cameron was on the landing. He descended as he spoke. "Is there something you want, Ned?"

The tone in his voice made Ned feel as welcome in the house as an ant at a picnic. "It's Molly I've come to see."

"Molly's not receiving visitors today." Cameron, now at his side, took him by the elbow to escort him out.

"Ned?"

He turned to see Molly at the head of the stairs, a baby in arm. He brushed past Cameron and rushed the stairs two at a time.

"Molly, I..." Suddenly, he didn't know what to say.

"Why don't we talk in here?" She led him into her room.

Ned closed the door behind him, then opened it again. He'd never been in a proper woman's room before and wasn't certain what *was* proper.

"Close it," she told him as she sat in the rocker.

She patted the crying baby's back. Ned walked to the cradle and gingerly picked up the other crying baby.

"Molly I... well, ah." His tongue seemed swollen, too big to work in his mouth.

The rocker was going faster and faster. Suddenly, it stopped. Molly looked up at him. "Ned, I'm marrying Mr. Page today."

Ned clung tighter to the baby, uncaring of her wetness which was mingling with his sweaty shirt. He paced the floor, patting the baby lightly on the back. But mostly he was trying to think of what to say.

"I want to thank you for all you have done to help us."

He tried to crush down his feelings. He felt such hopelessness, like being in quicksand with nothing to cling to. "Molly, I..." They were empty, clumsy words. He went to the window and looked down at Page's man. "Why are you doing this?" He turned and walked toward her. "I thought...well, er...I thought—" He couldn't bring himself to say that he thought she had feeling toward him. "You didn't like Page."

"I..." She got up and crossed to the bed where she laid Ruth down. "That was before I realized what a wonderful man he was."

Even with sweat running down his chest and back, he felt a chilled hand clutch his heart. Having the hose pulled out from under him wouldn't have surprised him more. There wasn't one ounce of niceness in Page's over-stuffed body. How could she think him wonderful?

Molly started changing the baby. "He's giving the three children a nice home, Ned. Not every man would be willing to take on three orphans."

Ned held the baby to his cheek. He wanted to tell her he would, but the words wouldn't form. It was just as well, what could he offer them? A log cabin isolated in the mountains was not equal to the Circle 8 spread. Probably starve come winter.

He cleared his throat to send back down his pounding heart. Ned suspected this had more to do with Cameron's wanting that money than Page's kindness. Perhaps if he could stall her and ride to town and ask Miss Alma what to do. "What about your aunt? You're not waiting for her return?"

Her hands froze on the diaper pin. "You give her a message for me, please. Tell her she's welcome anytime at the Circle 8."

Ned wondered how welcome Miss Alma would be once the unvarnished truth was known. Up until now he thought it might not matter to Molly, but now he realized he didn't know her at all.

Molly dropped the soiled diaper in the pail. "Hyeh, you take Ruth now and give me Naomi," Molly said as she thrust Ruth into his arms.

His heart was being faster than a runaway team. "Molly, I..." Ned crossed to the window at the sound of horses. "Timmy's back."

She sighed. "Good. Wouldn't do to keep Mr. Page waiting."

Ned nodded though he didn't agree. "No, reckon not."

"Will you see to the cradles, Ned?"

Ned bobbed his head. He worked his way around the bed to the cradles. Somehow carrying out the cradles gave a finality to their going. If the first cradle took a while to get down to the rig, it wasn't nothing to what the second one took.

When Ned returned from the final trip, the babies were bundled tightly in blankets.

Molly looked around the room. "Guess that's everything." Her eyes fell on the pail of wet diapers.

"I'll get it," Ned assured her.

Ned picked up the bawling baby, leaving the quiet one for her, then stooped down and took the handle of the pail. He got a good whiff of ammonia in the bargain.

A flutter of a feeling made it important to know which baby he was holding. He liked this little lady; somehow her bawling made them soul mates.

On the stairs, he asked; "You think even their ma could tell them apart?"

She smiled. "Sure she could. I can."

He stopped, one foot on the next step, and looked at the baby in her arms, and then at his. "Look the same to me."

"Look at Naomi's right ear." She flipped her head toward the one he held.

Ned placed the pail on the step and gave the wee one a hard look around the ear.

"The other right ear," Molly added with glee.

He gently put his finger on her cheek to turn her head to see the other side, but she whirled back toward him and grabbed his finger in her mouth.

He gave a little shriek of surprise as he jerked back. Molly turned away and Ned could see her shoulders jumping up and down with laughter. He could feel his hot face burn even brighter.

When they were at the bottom of the stairs, Molly shoved Ruth into his arms after she took Naomi. Pulling the blanket down, she said, "See the little freckle?" He leaned over for a hard look. "Ruth has one on the left ear." He looked hard at the other one, but wasn't about to put his finger anywhere close.

The mood of gaiety suddenly sobered as they stepped through the door. Timmy was half-heartedly playing mumblety-peg by the corral with Shorty, well away from the wagon. Molly took the pail and slipped the second baby into the crook of his arm. "Wait here a minute."

Ned stayed back in the shade of the porch. She dropped the pail in the back of the wagon then quickly walked toward the boy. It didn't take much more than horse-sense to recognize the disappointment on the little tyke's face as she

126

bent down and spoke to him.

Timmy ran toward the house, slowed and, keeping his eyes peeled on Ned as though he expected him to do something, disappeared inside.

Ned watched Molly speak to Shorty for a moment, no doubt thanking him. On her way back, she stopped to ask the driver to carry the little calf in the barn to the wagon.

Cameron, sitting next to the driver, looked up. "Sun's getting high in the sky."

Molly gave him a look that could send a snake into hibernation, but said nothing. She made her way back to the porch. "Ned, thank you for being so kind and all." She took Naomi.

The thanks embarrassed him. "I'm only sorry your aunt missed you." He thought it best to keep twisting the truth, the unvarnished facts would be out soon enough.

Molly smiled. "Well, it's a shame Cameron's going back without seeing her. I'm sure eventually I'll meet her. Though, surely, the twins will keep me pretty busy for quite awhile."

Timmy came back dragging a bundle tied inside a shirt.

Molly took a long, deep breath. "Well, thank you again." The Circle 8 hand appeared with the calf. "We're taking the calf. I'll see that Rocking J gets it back next year."

Ned didn't know how to say it. "Molly, I—"

"Molly, for Pete's sake, come on," Cameron called, spooking the team. The driver, who had just made room for the calf, had to run around the wagon and grab the lines to rein the team in. He gave Cameron a long, disgusted look. So did Ned.

"I have to go, Ned." Biting down hard on her lip, Molly turned and walked toward the wagon. Timmy followed like he was going to his own hanging. Ned caught up with him.

Ned took back Naomi as Shorty helped Molly into the wagon. The two men in the front seat didn't seem to notice that a little help would have been appreciated.

Dread came to Ned like a splash of cold water on a winter's

morning. When Timmy sat down next to her, Ned handed them each a baby. He'd barely moved back before the driver started the team. All the way out the yard, only Timmy looked back.

"Well now if that don't beat all!" Shorty piped up. "Cain't understand why she'd do such a tomfool thing." He cut his eyes to Ned like he expected him to do something about it.

"Reckon some people are more impressed with money than others," Ned said as he kept his eye on the wagon.

Shorty scratched his head. "That Cameron fella's the sorriest excuse for a human being. He I can see liking Page, but the girl, now that I just cain't figger. She seemed so...nice."

"Maybe we just didn't know her all that well."

Shorty's whiskers worked back and forth. "Women are shorly the strangest of critters."

They continued to follow the wagon with their eyes until distance swallowed it up.

Chapter Twenty-Five
Doc

Doc slowed his buggy to allow the galloping horse passage. He whoa'd the team when Yates was at his side.

"Mornin'," the doc said as he waited for his flush-looking friend to catch his breath. "Looks like a nice one today."

Yates nodded his howdy. "Shorly does," Yates finally managed. "Where ya headed, Doc?"

Doc took off his hat and ran his fingers through a scant thatch of hair. "Rocking J. Want to look in on the twin babies." He rubbed his greasy fingertips together. "Have some nursing bottles for them."

Yates shook his head. "Sad state of affairs. First the father's accident, then the mother." He sucked air through the gap between his front teeth. "Why in tarnation do these squatters leave their kin back east to come to this country to live like poor church mice?"

"Thought the grass was greener." They both looked around at the green landscape, which would soon be blanched white by the burning summer sun.

"They were wrong about that. Dead wrong."

Doc, noticing how proud Yates was of his little pun, chuckled as he wrapped the ends of the reins around the whip. He got out of the buggy and stretched his legs. He crossed the road and pulled up a stem of grass. The taste of rain clung to it.

Yates dismounted and picked a grass stem and bit down on it. "You haven't been here long. What brought you west, Doc?" He showed green-stained teeth.

Doc rubbed his own. "My health. It's dryer here."

Yates nodded like he understood. He didn't. A duel, long outlawed in the States, gone wrong brought him. He was a Masonic brother's second in a dispute over the honor of his woman. He had tried to stop his brother, but in the end was forced to replace him. Damp prison cells are unhealthy.

"Seeing as though you're goin' out to the Rocking J anyways, reckon you could take along this letter?" He reached up into a pouch on the pommel of the saddle and pulled out a letter. "For Ned. From the law firm in Kansas City that's always sending letters. Usually save 'em up until someone's in town, but this one has urgent written on it."

"Certainly."

"Save me a trip."

The doc took the letter and put it in his breast pocket. "No sense in both of us going."

"That's the way I seen it too, no sense both us goin'." Relieved of his burden, Yates swung up into his saddle and turned back to town. "Thanks, Doc."

"Don't mention it." Doc clicked the team into motion. He took in the quiet scenery. The ride promised to be a peaceful one, and he had plenty of time. No babies to be born for several weeks, and with the new Chickasaw cure-all he didn't expect anyone would be looking him up for awhile. There was no better way of getting away than a ride in the country.

At a prairie dog town, Doc watched some of the little critters sunning themselves on their mounds while the younger ones played games of tag. Some merely watched his rig go by.

Working its way up, the sun got high enough in the sky for Doc's hat to provide shade. It became a real blessing.

Doc filled his notrils with the agreeable mixture of

sweet-brier, clover, and wild flowers as he looked to the west to gaze upon the royal purple Big Horns. The majestic mountains towered over the hundreds of miles of valley, little pockets of gold surrounded by green on the foothills. From the first of May, when buds appeared on the bushes, until about the first of July, when everything was burnt crisp, the plains could match anything New England had to offer. And nowhere else was the sky so big or so blue. So blue it hurt the eyes.

He stopped to listen to the yellow-breasted meadowlark sing its song on the sagebrush. The whinny of the team answered.

It was then that he noticed the smoke. Nothing was more dangerous than a prairie fire. It hadn't been but two seasons since the last one took the lives of two little brothers. Nesters. They were told to stay within the fire-ring surrounding the shack while their parents fought back the fire. The boys must have panicked as they saw the flames dance around them. Running away, they were consumed by the prairie fire when the leaping flames circled round and caught them going over a rise.

But it was too wet and green for fire season. On closer examination, Doc realized it was more likely a structure than a prairie fire. Slapping the lines, Doc prodded the team into a run.

A nester's place, Doc assured himself as he grew close. Doc furrowed his brows at the dozen or so carcasses of heifers scattered over the pasture, calves nudging their mamas. He headed up the path of the blazing shack just as the riders rode down.

All horses were reined in for the confrontation. A rider from the back flanked around the others. His left Zygomaticus major muscle was paralysed, giving an asymmetrical appearance to his face. As the man neared, Doc saw the spread incision. A jagged knife wound was the probable cause. "Reckon you best be goin' about your business."

Cold rage mixed with fright took full rein as Doc looked beyond the horsemen to the flaming shack. "Where are the folks who reside here?"

Brown juices dampened the dirt as one of the riders spat. "Burnin' in Hell by this time, most likely," he said, wiping his mouth with the back of his left hand.

The leader gave the man a glacial stare.

Doc jumped down and started toward the burning structure.

Out of the corner of his eye, Doc saw one of the men shake loose a rope. Doc kept on going. The man twirled it above his head and sent the loop sailing. Doc jerked from his feet as the slack was pulled up. Spurring the horse away, his assailant pulled him completely around and flopped him hard on his backside, knocking out his breath.

Doc's glasses went flying as he was dragged. The rope swung wide, flinging him into a fence post, then back into a wheel of his own rig, where he caught a horse's kicking leg in the middle of his back. It was all happening so fast he hardly had time to comprehend the pain.

The dragging went on in what seemed an endless nightmare. With all his failing strength, Doc grabbed the rope and managed to lift the top half of his body off the ground, but not before his face and chest were skinned and covered with stickers. Bouncing off the corner fence pole, Doc flipped over on his back and was forced to turn loose of the rope as the heads of both humerus bones pulled from their sockets.

He felt the warmth of his own blood run off his face as he tasted the dirt in his mouth. A blur of excitement surrounded him. Vaguely he became aware of a mixture of noises: fleeing horse hooves, jeers and laughter, catcalls, and blood pounding in his ears.

Doc sucked dirt and blood, his eyes blinded by dust particles. He flip-flopped behind the running horse over and over again. For a fleeting moment he worried about the letter he promised to deliver to the Rocking J. It was an obligation he couldn't keep. Numbness set in and at last he smelled the all-too-familiar scent of death.

Chapter Twenty-Six
Molly

The trip was hot and dusty. The babies vacillated between fussy and lethargic. Molly's arms ached from the continual holding of one and sometimes two babies. During the few times when both babies slept, Molly insisted on holding them. Timmy's small frame surely ached more than hers. Both of them had contorted their bodies all the long day in order to keep the babies in the shade.

She should have been able to work herself into a real tizzy, but instead was caught up in some sort of insane euphoria. It started when she accidentally touched Ned's rock-hard arm when she took one of the babies from him. Something in their closeness, so close Molly could smell saddle soap, made her stomach quiver. Strange she should find saddle soap so appealing.

Molly knew she had to snap out of it. Today was her wedding day. Fine thing, thinking about another man on her wedding day, she chastised herself.

Somehow she had hoped Ned would ride up on a white stallion, dressed in armor like the knights from the fairy tales she learned at her mother's knee, and rescue her. Though why she thought such an absurd thing was more than she could fathom.

Cameron found countless things to complain about, but

made a special point of making his irritation with the babies' crying known. Did he think the fussy babies bothered neither Timmy nor her? Did he think Timmy and she enjoyed listening to the baying calf? In truth, Molly would have enjoyed making her irritation of Cameron's less-than-helpful attitude known. He was the one going home to see his dreams realized, while Molly expected only nightmares.

"Look, Timmy." Molly nodded to a bald eagle perched on a fence post. It rose on clumsy wings and then soared regally over the field.

Timmy twisted, following the eagle's flight.

The driver spat brown phlegm over the side, but the wind splattered it back on Molly. "Nesters. What right have they to fence in open range?"

Molly held her tongue.

The sun vanished behind the Big Horns, casting a sliver of deep red light over the mountain range. Molly felt a chill, either from the bleakness of the sudden darkness or from the urine soaking through the blankets and her skirts.

"Sonny," she called to the driver. "Could you please stop a minute?"

"Only a couple of miles to go. Still want'a stop?"

"No." Molly wanted to change the babies, or get out the heavier blankets if nothing else. She turned to Timmy. "Hyeh, let me have her. Hop over the seat and hunt for their other blankets, please."

Timmy crawled over the back, delivering a glancing blow to Molly's neck as his foot hurdled the back of the bench.

She gave a little shriek, stirring Cameron as well as the two babies.

"I'm sorry, Molly," Timmy said, greatly concerned.

Cameron, an arm resting on back of the front seat, spun around. "What's wrong with you, boy? Didn't you hyeh the driver say we're almost theyh? Can't ya sit still?"

Timmy started to sniffle.

Molly shot daggers at the back of Cameron's head. "I'm all right, Timmy. It didn't hurt, just startled me." Her voice was harsher now. "Cameron, the child's finding heavier blankets for the babies. It's cold now, or hadn't you noticed, Brother dear?"

Cameron ignored her.

When Timmy was back with blankets, they switched the babies back and forth until they were wrapped. The jerking motion of the wagon helped rock them to sleep.

The howling of coyotes on the hilltop put the finishing touch to the ride. Molly was almost glad to see the outline of the big dark house against the night's stars.

Inviting light spilled from the windows and the scent of burning pine hung in the air. No one was there to greet them as they pulled into the yard. Cameron knocked on the door, which was soon opened by a little Chainaman. Warmth rushed into the darkness.

"Wong," Cameron uttered as he stepped in.

The man bobbed his head as each of the visitors stepped inside. "Follow me, please."

Cameron stepped right along. Molly juggled the baby with one hand as she combed her fingers through Timmy's hair. She licked her fingers to smooth down his cowlick. "You're a mighty handsome fellow, suh." Taking a deep breath and straightening her back, Molly added, "Lets go." She walked resolutely into the library and headed toward the crackling fireplace, Timmy half-hidden behind her skirts.

Page struggled out of one of the black leather couches, a cigar centered between his teeth. He pulled out the cigar with a twirl. "Cameron, so nice to see you." He clasped him on the back hard enough to send dust flying. They walked a couple of steps to the other couch. "It is an honor to introduce Judge Jefferson Hodges. My young friend, Cameron Stewart."

The elderly judge was little more than skin stretched over

a frail skeleton. His dull eyes were set deep in their sockets. He lifted a bony arm like the Grim Reaper pointing the way. Cameron shook his hand and clawed nervously at the rash on his neck.

Page moved to the warm fireplace where he put a loving arm around Molly. Molly smelled liquor on his breath before choking on the cigar smoke as he turned her to face the judge. "And this here's my bride, Miss Molly. Cameron and Miss Molly are the new owners of the Rocking J."

Molly whipped around. "But... but that's not—"

Cameron was at her side. "Molly, let me help you with the children."

Her eyes shot to Cameron. Now it was crystal clear why Page was so eager to marry her.

"Wong, come take this baby from Mrs. Page." Page gave an unsteady smile. "The soon-to-be Mrs. Page."

She looked at the drunken cattleman. It was quite obvious that Page and the judge had been fortifying themselves for the big event. Molly glared at Cameron. As much as she disliked Page, she detested Cameron more. Molly didn't want to be in the same room with any of them. "Why don't I just take the children along? They have to be fed and bedded down." She gave Timmy a reassuring smile, though the reason for encouragement eluded her.

"Hurry right back. Jefferson has to leave early in the morning. I had to twist his arm to stay this long."

"Now, Franklin, that's not true."

That wasn't the only thing that wasn't true, Molly mused to herself.

"Nothing I like better than presiding over weddings. But I do need to leave bright and early in the morning. Have a trial up in Sheridan day after tomorrow."

"Maybe you could give me a hand, Brother dear." Molly managed the slightest smile as she left the room behind the Chinaman.

Wong led them upstairs and stopped at the first door. "Your room, Missy Page."

The name sent shivers down her spine. She walked in. Sonny had brought up their things, including the cradles. Tired and cranky, Molly was thankful for a place to sleep. She wanted nothing more than to curl up on the bed.

Instead, she went to the bed and stripped the soaking clothes off the first baby. Timmy laid the other one down beside her. "And the next room is Timmy's?" she asked Wong.

Wong fingered his black silk Mandarin collar. "Mr. Page said in bunkhouse with boys."

"No!" Molly said firmly. "I need his help with the babies."

"Make up new room right 'way," he said, bobbing his head.

"Why don't you do that?" Cameron pushed him toward the door. "And take Timmy with you to help."

Timmy turned his eyes up to Molly. Molly smiled and nodded. "You go on and get some fresh milk for your sisters."

When they were gone, Cameron whispered. "Molly, I need this money."

Molly was angry and tired, and didn't trust herself to say anything civil. "Will you stop at nothing?" She looked around the room. "Bring me the diaper cloth pail." She pointed it out. "And the pitcher and basin. That man doesn't want me, he wants the Rocking J."

"Keep your voice down."

"You have to tell him, Cameron. He's going to find out." She threw the soaking wet clothes in the pail. She poured water into the basin to clean the fussing baby.

"The agreement I have with him is the money for the marriage. That's all."

She dug night clothes out of one of the trunks. "but you know now why he wants me. He told the judge right in front of us and we didn't deny it. That's fraud."

"It won't matter when you're married." He was at her side pleading.

"It will to me!" she hissed as she picked up the clean baby. "Rock her."

Cameron sat in a cane rocker. "Keep pretending that the Rocking J belongs to your Aunt Missy. You can tell him—"

Molly's hand froze. "Pretend?"

Cameron leaned his head against the back of the rocker and howled. "Oh, of course, you don't know." He got up and carried the baby stiffly back to her. "Our precious Aunt Missy's the madam of a whorehouse. Isn't that rich?"

Molly continued dressing the baby.

"What do you say to that, Molly dear?" he whispered in her ear as he laid the crying baby on the bed.

"How do you know?" she tried to keep her voice natural.

"Easy enough. Page and I went to her place...for a drink...the night of the box social. She's the spitting image of Aunt Carrie. And besides you, she's the tallest woman in the whole wooly West. Page was so drunk that his mouth overran with information. Jennings wasn't married. This was all an elaborate hoax for our benefit."

"I suspect you can hardly wait to get back home to tell everyone."

"What! And have my friends find out we have a soiled dove in our family tree? No, her secret's safe enough. As long as you keep quiet." Cameron ran his hand over her shoulder. "I'll leave in the morning with the bank draft, you just keep pretending until it's had a chance to clear. You don't want our dear Mama to end up in the poorhouse, now do you?"

Cameron slipped out of the room without waiting for her answer. Molly sat on the bed between the crying babies and wept.

After the children were fed and bedded down, Molly put

on her finest gown and joined the men in the library. The three of them were having a great ol' time.

"Molly, dear," Page said, rushing to her and dragging her back like a reluctant calf being cut from the herd. "Well, Judge, by the fireplace?"

The judge, as if remembering his duty, picked up the Bible, rose and tottered to the fireplace to join them. Cameron, drink in hand, walked over and stood behind the bride and groom and leaned a casual arm against the mantle.

Molly only half-listened to the words the judge was trying to read with his liquor-glazed eyes. She concentrated instead on what this meant to Cameron and her mother, and the three children.

Soon it was over, a half-maudlin laugh came from her throat as her husband missed her lips in an attempt to kiss the bride.

Cameron kissed Molly, shook Page's hand, then the judge's. "Judge, if you wouldn't mind, I'd like to ride along with you as far as French Creek. It's time I headed back East."

Chapter Twenty-Seven
O'Malley

O'Malley tagged Ned as being out of sorts the minute the foreman walked into the bunkhouse. A wood shaving from the block he was whittling was on his boot. Ned knocked it and the boot half-way across the aisle as he passed.

"What you do that for?"

Ned kept walking.

O'Malley decided it was an accident. "What do you think, Ned?" He held up the wood carving.

Ned picked up the greasy kerosene lantern to have a closer look. "Too early to tell."

O'Malley frowned. "It's a horse for Timmy."

"Timmy's gone."

"Gone?" O'Malley got up and followed him to his bunk.

Ned flopped down and stretched out.

"What do you mean gone?"

"Miss Stewart is marrying Page and the children went with her."

O'Malley's mouth opened wide enough for a fly to circle in. He turned to Shorty, expecting wisdom to spout from the old toothless man. Shorty turned over on his bunk and buried his head under the pillow.

"How could you let her do that?" O'Malley demanded of Ned.

"Don't see where it had anything' to do with me."

The boy didn't understand how the foreman could be so calm about it. There was lots he could have done. "I thought you and she...well I thought...."

"Guess you thought wrong."

Angered, O'Malley flipped the blade of his knife, sending it across the room and into the splintered pine wall. "Dammit, man, what about Timmy? You jist goin' let Page mold his thinkin'!"

Ned put his arms under his head, his eyes looking straight up. "If you don't like the way I run things here, maybe you should go to Page, too."

The block horse slipped from his hands. A cold knot drew tight across his gut. He had worked for Page and would never do it again. Now Ned was telling him he wasn't welcome at the Rocking J. The Rocking J was home to him. He had nowhere else to go. Page ran the only other big outfits in the area. He'd have to quit French Creek. "I'll get my plunder together."

O'Malley knew every man there was feigning sleep, not a sound was heard. Usually they snored like the Dickens. He dug his knife out of the wall.

"I'll see that your pay finds it way to the Circle 8."

"Pay me now. I wouldn't work for an outfit like the Circle 8."

"And take that gelding you're so fond of with you to the Circle 8."

O'Malley turned and looked at him hard. He didn't own a horse of his own, but it didn't make a lick of sense that Ned would give him a Rocking J horse. The boys started snickering, then he saw the smile on Ned's face. O'Malley's spirits lifted clean to the roof. He understood. He was to go to the Circle 8 and watch over Molly and the younguns. "What if Page won't have me back?"

"Don't go borrowing trouble."

O'Malley nodded. "Got enough to go around as it is."

Chapter Twenty-Eight
Injun

The invaders rode long and hard. The wheels of the covered wagon moved so fast the spokes reeled as one. They pushed north.

As the new men neared the county line in a cloud of smoke, Injun cut the telegraph wires. Thus the invasion began.

This had not been one of Injun's better days. Felt out of sorts with a head threatening to explode. He reckoned it was tied to the medicine that Quaker sold him. If he weren't already dead, Injun would be thinking seriously about making him so again.

Their small party had pretty well started the ball rolling. Injun guided the new men while the others worked at convincing every nester in the valley to find a better place to settle. Starting with the south side, working north.

They labored under the theory that scaring the women folk went a long way in convincing the nesters to move on. Not long after, wagons, loaded to the sky, were on all roads leading out of the county.

Chapter Twenty-Nine
Townsfolk

The streets of French Creek were jammed with homesteaders trying to get the sheriff's attention. A range war was building in the valley. Barbed wire was coming down at an alarming rate. Blood had turned the valley red. But it wasn't until a homesteader brought in Doc's body that the town took a side.

Doc's funeral was held the next afternoon in the Willow Grove Cemetery just south of town. Not an establishment was open during the afternoon as the members of the Masonic Lodge marched in solemn procession, their white aprons fluttering in the spring breeze.

The mourners wavered between heartsick and seething mad. Not only was the doc well-liked, but he was needed. Doctors were scarce in the West. They had been lucky to have him. His death was a big blow to the whole community. And, bushwhacked the way he was, any one of them could have been in that coffin instead.

Doc had been dragged, then shot in the back. Only a hardcase could have done him that way. And it didn't take a scholar to realize the problems started with the arrival of Page's new hands. A bad lot if there ever was.

The willows swayed overhead as the tophatted, gloved, and aproned Worshipful Master Duncan and his Brothers began the graveside services. Everyone solemnly looked on as the livery owner started.

"From time immortal it has been the custom of Ancient Free and Accepted Masons to accompany the body of a Brother to the place of internment and there to deposit the remains with the usual formalities." Duncan continued his rote speech remembering the time Doc set his leg after a spooked horse's kick snapped the bone. Doc came running, a Rainbow dangling at the end of his fishing line. When Duncan finished, he dropped a sprig of evergreen in the grave and said, "Alas, my brother."

Yate's voice left him when it came his turn. If only he had ridden along with Doc instead of asking him to take the letter for him. Maybe if he had gone, Doc would be alive today. On the other hand, he himself may have been planted next to Doc. The sprig sailed down, splashing over where Doc's decaying face rested under the pine box. "Alas, my brother."

The sheriff rubbed the sprig between the fingers of his white cotton glove until it stained green. He would miss Doc. Doc had been his confidante. And drinking with him had been something akin to a spiritual experience. The sprig twirled down and bounced off the pine box. "Alas, my brother."

The mayor stepped up. His daughter was awaiting her first blessed event under the care of the good doctor. *Who would care for her now?* Mayor Tully wondered as he looked down into the hole in the earth. Killing the doc was a big, big mistake. The sprig fell in the crack between the pine box and the cold dirt. "Alas, my brother."

Thaddeus, the undertaker, shuddered remembering how bad Doc looked. Took hours to clean him up. Blood and dirt mingled like that. The only thing not ripped to shreds was the blood-stained letter Yates come looking for. "Alas, my brother."

Gentry stared hard at the coffin. He was hoping to get a message beyond the grave as to what should be done with Doc's bank account. Maybe no one would come forward to claim it. "Alas, my brother."

Quietly the black-banded mourners walked in family groups down the hill to the motley group of wagons, buckboards, buggies and saddle horses. After seeing their families safely home, every man headed to The Egyptian for the emergency town meeting.

Chapter Thirty
Alma

Out of courtesy to the respectable women of French Creek, Alma made it her policy never to attend funerals. But she was at the saloon when the meeting started.

Mayor Tulley stood and clicked his beer mug with the stem of his pipe. "As elected Mayor of French Creek, I hereby open this meeting." He waited for silence. "As you know, our doctor has been brutally murdered. Shot in the back by assailants unknown."

A voice from the back interrupted him. "We know all that. What we wanta know is what the law's going to do about it."

As with one voice the room roared.

The mayor sucked on his pipe. He slid it to the side of his mouth. "Well, Sheriff, what are you going to do?"

Someone out of Alma's sight spoke up. "There's no question as to who they are. Page's men."

Another added, "Page's foreman, that Saint fella is riding with them."

Others voiced like sentiments.

Being the town's best scratcher, the sheriff started in. He scratched his head, then his neck, bent over to scratch the left knee, then tugged at an ear. "Reckon we should get up a posse and go round up these men." He was big on getting up posses.

Heads bobbed.

Alma stood and worked her way toward the head table. She waited to speak until a hush came over the room. "Sheriff, it will take more than a posse. One of my girls was told there's twenty-two hired guns."

Grady yelled, "There's more than twenty-two of us. We can handle them."

He let whiskey do his talking too often, but when others cheered in agreement Alma realized that God had short-changed more than one of them. "They're *all* gunslingers." The men seemed to noticeably shrink in their chairs. The sheriff commenced to scratch. When he started in on his crotch, Alma added, "Think you should throw in with the hands from the Rocking J. This concerns all of us."

In a lick, Duncan was out of his chair and shouting; "The Rocking J will back the other two spreads. They always stick together."

Alma yelled over the clamor. "That's not so. Mr. Jennings was the first to stand up for the cause of right. You think Ned Lawson won't?"

"Don't matter what Ned wants," Duncan added, "one of the new owners married Page yesterday. Reckon that makes Page family."

Alma grabbed the side of the table for support as her knees buckled. "Married? You sure?"

"Sure I am. Talked to the judge. His horse threw a shoe," he added as validation. "Reckon he knew since he married them and all. He'd just left the brother at the stage. Reckon that makes Page in charge of the Rocking J."

Murmurs rose through the saloon. Alma pulled a chair and sat.

"Counting all the hands, there's a peck of them. We should send a wire to Fort McKinny," Gentry offered.

Yates was standing next to the batwing door. "Can't. Wire's down."

Thaddeus rose. "I make a motion that the sheriff rides to the fort."

"I second that," was heard in unison in at least eight different voices.

Mayor Tulley got in just ahead of the sheriff. "All those in favor?"

A roar of ayes followed.

"All opposed?"

The sheriff looked as if he would have liked to.

Alma didn't stay to hear anything else.

Chapter Thirty-One
Ned

Ned squinted into the westerly sun. The Circle 8 loomed ahead in the distance. Spurring his horse into a run, Ned fingered the blood-soaked letter in his pocket.

If he'd read it once, he'd read it a hundred times. It didn't make a lick of sense. Why would anyone give him the Rocking J? The one thing he did know, once Molly had the nursing bottles, he'd make sure Page read the letter. Perhaps he could put a stop to all the shenanigans the way Jennings would have if he were still alive.

The light had emptied from the sky by time Ned rode into the yard. Ned led the horse to a lope. He braced himself as he walked to the door and knocked.

A nervous Chinaman cracked the door.

"Miss...Mrs. Page, please."

He looked cautiously around the foyer behind him. Leaning his head around the door, he whispered, "In the barn."

Ned could hear Page ranting and raging in the background as the Chinaman slammed the door closed. He doubted Page's disposition would improve once he'd read the letter. The letter could wait until after he'd visited Molly. He had to make sure she was doing all right. He couldn't help worrying about her, even though she was another man's wife. And when he tried hard not to, a pain in his gut reminded him how he'd failed all of them. Miss Alma, Molly and the children.

A silhouette in the failing light, Molly sat on a stool, milking the lone cow.

Ned was assaulted by so many quicksand feelings. He wanted to seize her up, throw her across his saddle, and hightail-it away. Instead he asked; "Where's Timmy?"

Her head whirled around fast enough to send sparks of light flying. Molly turned back just as quickly. "He's with Red. They're finding a ma for the calf. It was taking to this one heyh, but the babies need all this."

"O'Malley working here now?"

She shook her head, never looking up.

"No?" He walked closer. Her face was swollen and discolored. This was Page's doing, he was certain. He knelt down and cupped her chin. Her eyelids were puffy from crying. "What's happened to your face?"

She pulled away. "I have to get some milk for the babies."

Despair threaten to overtake him. He was a law-abiding citizen, but his strong sense of justice told him that, in this instance, man's law was a far cry from just. He simply didn't see what he could do about it. Ned put the box down beside her. "The nursing bottles came. They brought them to the Rocking J."

"Thank you." The silence was foiled only by the squirting milk splashing into the bucket.

"What happened with O'Malley?"

"Got in a fight with Page. Something about stealing a Rocking J horse."

Ned's eyes were unfocused on the stream of milk. "Surprised they didn't lynch him."

"I pleaded with Page to leave him alone until they found out for sure. For Timmy's sake." She shrugged her shoulders. "Page was strange after that. Told him he could stay as long as he liked provided he kept Timmy in tow...and for no pay."

151

"Page beat you?" Her silence was answer enough. "How come?"

"Because of the lie!" came the answer at the entrance of the barn. The teetering Page stood swinging a lantern. "They lied to me!" He stumbled forward. "They don't own the Rocking J at all."

"No, I own the Rocking J." Ned took the letter from his pocket as he started toward him.

"You?"

The brown crusts of blood flaked as Ned unfolded the letter.

Page snatched the stiff paper. Weaving back and forth, Page held it to the light. The letter slipped from his hand.

Ned stooped to retrieve it.

Page roared with laughter as he backed up. "Jennings' heir *gave* it to *you!*"

"And I gave the horse to O'Malley."

Molly took the letter out of his hand.

Page laughed as he inched away. Abruptly his face contorted. He dropped the lantern and lunged at Ned.

Molly screamed.

Ned felt air gush out as Page toppled him. His hat went flying one way, as Page and he tumbled to the hay mat, Ned caught glimpse of a line of fire beyond the broken lantern. His hat had landed right smack in the middle of it and was on its way to being a memory. The barn was thick with the smell of kerosene. He had to put out the fire, and quickly. Ned struggled to move the fleshy arm at his throat so he could warn Page. The kerosense ignited with a shattering bang.

"Ned, stop. Fire." Molly ran to free the cow.

The irony of her words was not lost on him. He was caught under a good three hundred pounds of drunken lard, and she wanted him to stop? He pushed Page with everything he had. "Leave the cow," he said as he twisted free. Page rolled over and was out cold. The structure was too far gone to be saved. Ned turned his attention to Page. He took his feet and pulled hard. Wrestling a stubborn bull would have been easier. Embers caught Page's sleeve. Ned kept pulling, ever mindful of the rising flames around them.

Well out of the fire's reach, Ned dropped Page's feet. Something told him, had their roles been reversed, Page would not have extended the same curtesy. Molly was nowhere to be seen. He hurled a handful of dirt on the smoldering sleeve before running back into the barn to find her. The flames were jumping everywhere. "Molly, where are you?"

"Over here." Her voice rang out behind a screen of smoke. "The cow's afraid."

"The only critter in the barn with any sense." He found her. She had ripped off her skirt and wrapped it as a blindfold over the cow's eyes. White foam dripped from the cow's mouth as Molly tugged. "Go on out, I'll see to her." He pulled the reluctant cow as he watched Molly disappear through a wall of smoke. "Listen, sis," he struggled one-handed to get his bandanna over his nose, "we're going out whether you like it or not." The cow obeyed, crying when her split hooves caught burning hay. Ned held his breath nearly to the point of collapsing. Finally they were outside. Ned uncovered the cow's head and gave her a slap on the rear; she stampeded through the yard toward the corral of spooked horses.

Hands were running with bucketsful of water from the horse troughs, but the effort was akin to trying to spit out a campfire. Others slapped back the flames with saddle blankets. Page had come to and was being helped up by the Chinaman.

"The bottles!" Molly shrieked as she raced to the blazing barn.

"No! Leave them." His words were lost in the snapping of flames. Terror gripped him as he watched the roof sag under an orange ball of fire. His feet took flight of their own accord. In one swift motion, Ned vaulted through the flames and pushed Molly inside just as the timbers crashed down. They slid across the sweltering ground in each other's arms.

A wall of red flames cut off their escape. Smoke engulfed them like a shroud. They were going to die. He made a feeble attempt at wiping soot from her battered face with the tips of his blackened gloves. "Oh Molly, Molly. I love you so."

Her smoke-filled eyes sparkled for a second and a smile touched her lips. The smile vanished. "Then show some gumption." She scrambled to her feet. "There's a window in the granary that's been boarded up. I saw light pouring in between the slats this morning." Molly clutched his hand and led him through the blackness.

Smoke teared his eyes. But not so much that he didn't see the box of bottles when he stumbled over it. He jerked her back and picked them up. They were in this fix because of the bottles. He was going to save them or die trying! Even through the leather gloves Ned felt the blistering heat from the box, but he held fast.

With great trepidation they made it to the window. Molly started to pull at the boards. He handed over the bottles and with all his strength, kicked the boards. Molly's cough gave him added strength. His lungs were sizzling like hide to a branding iron. He wondered what hell was like if it could get this hot on earth, and was afraid he might find out sooner than he hoped. A board loosened on one side. It shot burning pain to his very soul as he bent it back for Molly. She squeezed through, gasping as a nail snagged her arm. The bent board snapped loose, knocking him off his feet onto the searing floor. He crawled to the opening and managed to scrape through.

"You're on fire!" Molly slapped the flames on his back with her bare hands.

He pushed her away, dropped to the ground and rolled in the dirt. Excitement gave way to calm when Ned finally realized they were safe. She was covered with soot from head to toe, her skirt was gone and her shredded petticoat would never be white again. He crushed her to him. "We're a sorry sight."

Molly laughed.

They rocked in each other's arms, watching the all-consuming blaze and smelling the toasted grain, like bread fresh from the oven. The flames abated, and then died out as the barn turned to ashes. Their escape route was a smoldering heap of blackened, parched grain.

"Come home with me," he whispered in her ear.

She stiffened, then wriggled out of his arms. "I'm another man's wife." Molly picked up the bottles and ran toward the house.

Ned saw the look of hatred on Page's face as Molly passed him. "Put on some clothing!" he bellowed. "Or was it your intention to have all the boys gawk at you?"

Molly gathered her petticoat close around her legs and hurried into the house, her head bent low.

For a split second, a look of disappointment came into Page's eye as Ned approached, out of the ashes. Page offered his hand. "Thank you for rescuing my wife."

Ned lifted an eyebrow. It took a selective memory on Page's part to foreget about being rescued himself. He shook the man's hand.

"Why don't you come along into the house and we can have a little chat about the valley?"

Ned wanted to have more than a chat, but he remembered how Jennings had always been so crafty in his dealings with Page. "Could use a drink, that's for certain."

Chapter Thirty-Two
Alma

Alma sequestered herself in her office. The gaiety that crept through the walls was as unwelcome as an uninvited guest. She poured another drink as she bent her head to the problem. Despite her slight-of-hand doings, Page had married her little Molly. The way she saw it, there was only one way to rectify the nefarious entanglement. Family protected family. After throwing the burning liquid down her throat, she reached in her desk drawer and pulled out the LeMat two-barreled revolver.

She ran her hand along the top barrel, remembering her brother's wide grin when he showed it to her after he and their father returned from a business journey to New Orleans. The eminent P.G.T. Beauregard had personally presented it to him. Not that Matthew knew in 1856 what an outstanding and acclaimed Confederate General Beauregard would become. But it meant the world to her to have this reminder of her respectable antebellum days. When it meant something to be gracious and hospitable.

Alma rummaged through the drawer looking for the box of ammunition. She kept the five-inch smoothbore barrel loaded with buckshot, which she had never actually used, but the nine-shot cylinder of the six-and-a-half inch barrel was always left unloaded. She tested the hammer, fitted with a pivoting striker, before filling the percussion revolver. She squeezed the checkered walnut grip with a vengeance.

Hoisting herself out of the chair, Alma swore revenge. She ripped her black cloak from the stand, threw it over her arm and opened the door. Page didn't know how to treat her girls right, a Southern young lady like Molly would be in perilous jeopardy. The gay laughter assaulted her. Joplin called to her as she walked by, but she ignored him.

Chapter Thirty-Three
Ned

The streets of French Creek were lined with nesters' wagons and buckboards piled high with belongings. Ned dropped the sheriff's body in front of The Egyptian. He dismounted and arched his back, working out the knots. He looked a sight. He felt naked without his hat. A stranger ran into the saloon with the big news. The ensuing ruckus caused a sizable gathering, everyone was asking questions.

"Found him at the fork of the Dry Gulch Road as I was headin' for town. Pumped full of lead, face down in the dirt."

Tulley looked down at the body. "He was heading for the fort to get the soldiers."

"What for?" Ned asked.

Ned learned the reason from a number of excited voices.

A nester spoke up. "I seen them working west on the county line...by that immigrant Kowaski's place."

These were not Page's regular hands, Ned gathered. Hired gunslingers from Texas, someone added. Ned squatted down beside the body. "Reckon you'll want us to form a posse if we're going to revenge you, Judd."

Tulley raised his voice over the noise. "As Mayor of French Creek, I appoint Ned Lawson as the newly appointed sheriff."

Ned jumped to his feet in protest, but his words were lost

in the cheers. He looked around and realized there wasn't much to be done about it. Seeing a Double D hand in the crowd, Ned said, "Charlie, ride to the Rocking J. Tell them to empty Jennings' gun case and meet us at the county line by Kowaski's place."

Charlie nodded and raced away.

"That there's a Double D hand. They'll stand with Page," came a voice in the circle.

Ned shook his head. "No, he's a good man, as are most of the Double D hands. They know right from wrong." Over the rumbling Ned hollered, "I'm deputizing anyone willing to ride with me. We'll leave at dawn...give the Rocking J men a chance to get there." Looking over the motley group, he added, "why don't you all turn in now?"

He mounted up as Tulley yelled, "Free firearms and ammunition to all deputies." Ned looked back over his shoulder to see the crowd of men hustling to Tulley's General Store. He would be along soon to buy a new set of clothes, but first he had other business.

Ned's blacken spurs jingled as he climbed the stairs to Miss Alma's—she was the reason he was on the road to town when he stumbled across the sheriff—and one bit into a raised board. Joplin rushed out from behind the bar when he saw Ned.

"Mister Lawson," the old man took a deep breath, "Miss Alma's gone, suh."

His luck was running true to form. "When will she be back?"

"You don't understand. She left...with the gun in her hand."

Ned looked beyond Joplin to the clients in the bar. "Anyone seen which way Miss Alma went?"

A teller from the bank propped his hand up like a schoolboy asking permission to go to the outhouse. Ned nodded to him. "Saw her heading over to the livery...like she was in a daze.

Had to move off the boards to let her pass."

"That was some iron she was toting," his friend added.

Ned turned on his heels, tore through the place, took the porch in two steps and jumped over the stairs. His horse crossed the French Creek bridge before Ned found his other stirrup. Ned's heel had barely slid up against it before he was dismounting and ground-hitching the horse in front of the livery. It was dark. He cupped his hands around his mouth and yelled up at the open window above and to the left of the livery. "Duncan? Duncan!" He called until the room grew light and he saw a shadow at the window.

"Can't a body get some sleep?"

"Duncan, it's me. Ned Lawson."

"So?"

"I'm looking for Miss Alma...you seen her?"

Duncan rubbed his eyes. "I seen her all right. Took her buggy and headed out to the Circle 8." Ned was on his horse before Duncan was able to say, "Had the strangest looking revolver I've ever laid eyes on. Wheeling it around she was..."

"Look, there goes Ned already." Ned vaguely heard someone call out as he galloped past Tulley's store.

Chapter Thirty-Four
Molly

"You're drunk." Molly leaned against the straining door. "Please...go to bed."

"I intend to," Page roared from the other side of the bedroom door, "with my bride."

Molly had managed to stay out of his bed so far and liked it that way. "Please, Mr. Page. You've wakened both babies. I need to feed them now."

Through the door she heard light footsteps on the stairs.

"What is it, Wong?"

"Mr. Page, Mr. Page, a buggy."

The lamp by Molly's bed flickered as Page gave the door a final decisive blow. Molly ran to the window and looked out. The nearly full moon illumiated Aunt Missy as she stepped down from the buggy. Before Molly had a chance to ask herself why she was here, another rider galloped into view. It was Ned! Molly grabbed her shawl from the rocker and ran for the door.

Page's palms were spread out in front of him. With every step Aunt Missy took toward him, he took a step back. He felt for the step with the heel of his boot as he looked down the barrel of the heirloom LeMat revolver. "Now, Miss Alma. You don't know what you're doing."

"Miss Alma," Ned said in a deep authoritative voice as he slid from his lathered horse. "Give me the gun, Miss Alma."

Aunt Missy inched forward.

Molly slipped out the door, her eyes focused on the LeMat. Wong stood beside her, shaking. She gathered the shawl tightly around her. "Aunt Missy, give Ned the gun."

With glazed eyes Aunt Missy looked at her over Page's head. "Aunt Missy?"

Molly watched Ned ease in on her. She would try to keep her distracted. "Aunt Missy, if you do this, you're no better than he is. Hand the gun over to Ned."

"Miss Alma, I'm the new sheriff and I'm taking Page in. I'll see that justice is done."

The LeMat wavered. "New sheriff?"

Ned reached out but she jerked the revolver back.

"Judd's dead. Found him on the road by the fork."

Her laugh was hideous. "The soldiers aren't coming now, are they?"

They both turned hearing the thunder of horses behind them. The Mayor at the lead.

Before Molly was aware, Page bent over and drew a Colt Derringer from his boot and cocked the hammer back.

"Look out!" Molly screamed.

Page shot.

Ned seized the revolver as it flew from Aunt Missy's hand. She clutched her wounded arm as she fell at Page's feet. Blood ran through her fingers. Dropping to his knee, Ned leveled the gun at Page. He fumbled with the hammer of the revolver. But it was a rifle report that doubled Page. He groaned and crumbled on top of Aunt Missy.

Furor reined. Townsmen clumsily dismounted side-stepping, rearing, whinnying horses, while the Circle 8 hands came running from the bunkhouse, which was clearly visible now that the barn was gone. Some of the hands were still dressing, tripping as they pulled on boots. Timmy and O'Malley were among them.

Tully and a couple of the other townsfolk leveled rifles at the throng of advancing Circle 8 hands.

"No!" Ned planted himself squarely between the two enraged factions. "Everyone ease back," he demanded. "There's no call for a fight. Our quarrel is not with you men. It's with the invaders been doing all the killing."

"Ours, too," one of the hands shouted.

Molly turned her attention to the knot of townsmen pulling Page off Aunt Missy.

"Is she dead?" Molly asked through a fear-parched mouth.

"Fainted." The man flipped Aunt Missy's cape over her shoulder. "Flesh wound."

"But he's dead," the man kneeling over Page stated vehemently.

Molly flinched. She despised Page, but wouldn't have wished death on him. "Page is dead, Ned," one of the men called out to him.

He nodded. "Page is dead, men. You're now working for Mrs. Page." He motioned for Molly to join him. "Any of you who thinks he can't take orders from a woman, or can't live beside a nester—"

"Homesteader," Molly corrected as she moved to his side.

"Homesteader...had better gather his plunder now."

None of them moved.

"The townsfolk and the Rocking J hands are joining forces to rid the county of Page's invaders. Any of you interested in coming along, saddle up."

Cheers went up as the men ran for the remuda and any guns they might have. Molly, keeping an eye on Aunt Missy, was relieved to see her sit up.

O'Malley stepped forward and greeted Ned with his open

hand. It warmed Molly to see them shake. "These men are still harboring ill-feeling from the shootists, as they call themselves, taking over some of their bunks. Chucked everything on the floor, they did."

"No way to make new friends." Ned advised O'Malley.

Molly bent to Timmy. "Let's go into the house now."

"I want to go with Ned."

Ned ruffled the boy's hair. "Plenty of time for night riding when you're grown. Need a good night's sleep in order to grow." He pointed him toward the house. "You're the man at the Circle 8, now."

Timmy walked tall beside Molly. They hurried into the house behind the man carrying Aunt Missy. Molly skirted round and directed him into the library. "Put her on the leather couch by the fireplace."

"Just put me down, Gayland. It was my arm hurt, not my legs."

Ned had followed them in and was leaning against the door-jamb watching Aunt Missy struggle free. Molly felt a deep heat on her face, recalling the things he said while they were in the burning barn.

"What happened to you, Ned?" Aunt Missy asked in the family's soft drawl as she fiddled with the bandanna bandage someone had wrapped around her arm.

"Page's barn burnt up." He sat beside Aunt Missy. "Molly, would you and Timmy excuse us for a moment?"

"Certainly," Molly said as she took Timmy's hand and lead him out. "Timmy, I forgot. Both of the babies were screaming when I left. Think you can help me with them?"

Timmy tripped on a leg of the Mahogany trestle table in the hall, spilling a vase of wild flowers he and O'Malley had pulled up for her. She caught the crystal vase, but not before water sloshed on the floor. Molly ran to the kitchen for a towel. Timmy was gathering up the flowers when she got back. She started soaking up the water. Although Ned and

Aunt Missy apparently hadn't heard the commotion in the hall for the ruckus in the yard, she couldn't help hearing them. Ned was telling her about the fire.

"Miss Alma, thank you for the gesture, but I can't take your ranch."

She laughed. "How'd you know?"

"You're the only one I know with a heart of gold big enough to give away a ranch."

Timmy looked questioningly at Molly. Molly held a finger to her lips. They shouldn't have been eavesdropping and she knew she should make their presence known, but she couldn't make herself do the right thing.

"Why'd you do it?" Ned asked.

"Many reasons. Thought it'd be the best way to save Molly from the likes of Page. After I learned what a skunk Cameron's turned out to be, I wanted to give it to Molly in a way he couldn't bleed her dry. Any fool can see that you two belong together. And, knowing you, you would never ask her to marry you as long as you were a hired hand." Molly's face felt crimson. Timmy had a wide grin on his face. "And I thought it'd be bad for business if folks knew I owned the ranch. Think I was getting too high-and-mighty. Keep my clientele away."

"Well, no one needs to know you own it. I'll stay on as foreman."

"You don't seem to understand, Ned Lawson. You own the Rocking J. Pay me back over time if you wish. But if I were you, I'd be looking at merging the two ranches before someone else gets the idea. You and Molly control the valley now."

Molly stuck the flowers in the vase.

"Don't forget the Duke."

"A real gentleman, the Duke. About time for one of his visits. Now, if you'll excuse me, suh, there's a couple of babies upstairs I'm anxious to see."

Molly took Timmy's hand and raced silently toward the stairs, the towel dragging behind.

"Looks like a whole bunch of my clients are out there waiting for you. Hurry up...you're ruining my business."

Chapter Thirty-Five
Injun

Injun saw the trail of dust despite the rising sun. The pounding of hooves shook the ground. He rode back to the sorry barn they had taken refuge in for the night. "Tom," he roared through the sleeping camp.

Tom rolled over in his blanket and looked down from the hay loft. "Better be important, Injun."

"Riders coming."

Tom rubbed his eyes. "How many?"

"Too many to count."

He sprang up and shouted orders to the sleepy men. Soon the whole camp stirred. "Get the wagon inside. We'll make our stand here."

Chapter Thirty-Six
Ned

Ned rode at the lead. It was a fool thing to do. He was unarmed and undetermined in his plans if trouble started. He thought to borrow Miss Alma's fancy gun, but decided it would take him days to work it, if he didn't shoot himself first.

They followed wagon tracks to Smyth's homestead just this side of Dry Creek, the southern boundary of the county line. Ned saw movement around the barn. He raised his hand, signaling a halt. The only noise he heard was the snorting and shuffling of horses. And the cocking of guns.

"Can you hear me in there?" Ned shouted.

An eternity of silence passed as they waited for an answer. Tulley struck a match and then blew it out, fouling the air with stench of rotten eggs. Ned watched him touch the hot tip to a tick in his horse's ear. They waited some more.

"I hear you."

"Page is dead. Take your choice. Ride out now, or face us."

Ned strained to hear the muffled voices in the barn, but couldn't hear anything over the sounds of shuffling hooves, coughing, and people trying to keep quiet.

"What do you feature they'll do, Ned?" Tulley asked as he flicked the tick to the ground.

Ned shook his head. "Have no idea. I still can't tell when cattle are going to stampede."

Tulley narrowed his eyes. "You *are* the sheriff, after all."

Ned fumbled in his pocket for his bag of tobacco. "That's another thing we need to talk about—"

"You out there." The voice bellowed from the barn.

He kneaded the sack black with soot from his gloves. "We hear you fine."

"Page dead?"

Ned stuck the tobacco in his pocket. As nervous as he was, he suspected he wouldn't be able to roll a decent cigarette. Didn't need every able-bodied man in the county to know. "Shot through the heart after shooting a lady."

"What lady?" a different voice asked. Saint's, Ned thought.

"That you, Saint?"

"It is."

"Miss Alma...Saint, can you see the Circle 8 hands behind me? They wouldn't dare be here if Page were still alive, would they?"

The silence wore on Ned. He felt for his tobacco.

"They sure are slow making up their minds." Tulley whispered.

Ned grunted. The slowness was giving him too much time to think. In some company their situation could be considered desperate. Twenty-two gunslingers forted up in a barn against fifty or sixty men armed with weapons they'd never fired before. The townsfolk part of the posse weren't much in the saddle, and were proving to be far more dangerous to each other than he suspected they'd be against the hired guns.

"You out there."

"Yeah?"

"We have your word we can go in peace?"

"Lynch them, Ned. Don't let the murdering bastards go free."

Ned eyed the man hard. "How much blood would be shed tryin'?"

The man mumbled something he couldn't hear.

Ned's heart pounded in his ears. He gave a warning look up and down the line. It would only take one shot, even an accidental one, to begin the bloodbath. "You have my word."

"We'll go then."

Ned drew a bated breath. So far the bluff had worked. It would be the biggest poker pot he'd ever won. He pushed his winning streak. "Saint, you and Blacky ride on out with them. It's time you quit these parts."

He motioned the cheering men to be silent. "They're not gone yet." The wagon started rolling flanked by riders. He was deaf to the excitement around him when the gang crossed the country line.

Tulley whacked Ned on the back. "Now, can I pick a sheriff or what?"

"I don't want to be sheriff."

"You have to be sheriff." Tulley looked wounded. "Where we going to find another?"

Ned shrugged. "Hire the man who shot Page. He knows his way around a rifle."

Tulley looked around. "Which one of you shot Page?"

Ned turned tail and clicked his horse into a canter. He had a more imporant question to ask.